IRENE SOLÀ is a writer and visual artist. She is the author of the novels *Dams, When I Sing, Mountains Dance* and *I Gave You Eyes and You Looked Toward Darkness*, and the poetry collection *Beast*.

MARA FAYE LETHEM is a writer, researcher and award-winning translator. Her recent translations include books by Irene Solà, Alana S. Portero, Jaume Cabré and Pol Guasch.

Also by Irene Solà and available in English

When I Sing, Mountains Dance

I GAVE YOU EYES AND YOU LOOKED TOWARD DARKNESS

Irene Solà

Translated from the Catalan by Mara Faye Lethem

GRANTA

Granta Publications, 12 Addison Avenue, London W11 4QR
First published in Great Britain by Granta Books, 2025
This paperback edition published by Granta Books, 2026

First published in the United States in 2025 by Graywolf Press, Minneapolis, Minnesota
Originally published in 2023 as *Et vaig donar ulls i vas mirar les tenebres*
by Editorial Anagrama

This book was translated with the help of a grant from the Institut Ramon Llull

A CIP catalogue record for this book is available from the British Library.

1 3 5 7 9 10 8 6 4 2

ISBN 978 1 80351 139 9 (paperback)
ISBN 978 1 80351 140 5 (ebook)

Book design by Rachel Holscher
Text set in Adobe Garamond Pro by
Bookmobile Design & Digital Publisher Services, Minneapolis, Minnesota
Offset by Iram Allam

Printed and bound by CPI Group (UK) Ltd, Croydon, CR0 4YY

The manufacturer's authorized representative in the EU for product safety is
BGC Sustainability & Compliance, 7 avenue du Général Leclerc, 75014 Paris, France
(gpsr@baldwinglobalconsulting.com).

www.granta.com

To Oscar

CONTENTS

Dawn 3

Morning 27

Midday 49

Afternoon 73

Evening 93

Night 111

Author's Note 157

Acknowledgments 161

I GAVE YOU EYES
AND YOU LOOKED
TOWARD DARKNESS

DAWN

gonosznak látszott, pedig csak öreg volt[*]

ANNA T. SZABÓ

The darkness was purple and fidgety, opaque, buzzing and speck-led, blind and thick, at once gleaming and fathomless. It was in-fested with worms, branches, tremors, veins, blotches. Impalpable stains formed the bulging walls of a room, its ceiling, a bed, a night table, a dresser, a door, and a window. The shadows crack-led. They vibrated, they murmured. They snored. The snoring was nasal, muffled and serrated. It grated, it gulped, and it choked. That rumbling emanated from the bed, and the bump that slept in the middle of it. An old woman. A portly old woman. Bernadeta's eyes were closed, her lizard lids lashless, her mouth open, her gossamer lips splotchy and lilac, her long, greasy hair splayed across the pillow. She was ugly. Or that's what the other woman, Margarida, was thinking as she sat beside her in a wicker chair, hands clasped in her lap, twiddling her thumbs.

---

[*] it looked evil, but was only old

In her bed, Bernadeta swallowed an ungainly exhalation, went quiet midway through a violent snore, and ceased breathing. Outside, owls sang, and then it was quiet. Margarida's thumbs stopped. She craned her neck and observed the old woman, and for a moment she thought that was it. That the time had come. But the dark chasm of Bernadeta's mouth sighed, inhaled, and the whole racket started up once more. Margarida again settled back in her chair and continued her twiddling. She was a puny woman with the head of a sparrow, severe eyes, a rigid mouth, lean cheeks, a parched throat, and curved shoulders. And she was praying. Poor Margarida prayed all through the night. Because the Lord commands us to pray and to bid others to pray. But since Margarida couldn't bid others to pray—because the tongues of her relatives, or at least those who had tongues, were mere lumps, incapable of saying anything helpful—Margarida prayed herself, in the hopes that, if she prayed hard and long, sooner or later God would hear her. Surely He would make out her voice amid all the sins and all the sinners. He would gather her up in His paternal arms, and He would say that He should never have abandoned her, *my daughter*, that Margarida was good and saintly, and that she was forgiven. Forgiven for the things she'd done, and the things the other women had done.

She prayed for those who weren't there. For those who'd gone and not come back. For her husband, Francesc. For her sons, Bartomeu, Esteve, and Guilla. And for her father, Bernadí. She didn't pray for Martí the Tenderhearted or Martí the Lame, for they were nothing to her. She prayed for the women of her house. For her mother, Joana, even though she was contemptible, and for her sister Blanca, even though she was deviant. For her niece, Àngela, even though praying for Àngela was a complete waste of time, and for her great-great-grandniece, Dolça, even though

Dolça should rot in hell and be heard shrieking down there below the stones, for being the daughter of whom she was the daughter of. She even prayed for Elisabet, who wasn't a relative of hers, but every Our Father she said for Elisabet counted triple. She prayed for Bernadeta too. But mostly she just watched over that old woman, who slept like a rotten fruit fallen from a tree. Because Margarida wanted to be there when Bernadeta died. And she wanted to see it. She wanted to watch as Bernadeta was denied divine grace and salvation for having had so many dealings with the devil.

Margarida had awaited death with exhilaration. Her own, that is. She'd imagined it would be a luminous flare, a spasm of glory, a conclusive joy, a smothering ecstasy accompanied by the sound of an army of angels playing lutes and trumpets. Hallelujah! Blessed be the designs of the Almighty! Praised be Our Creator! She had glimpsed it so many times in her mind's eye that it was as if it had already happened. The gates of heaven opening to welcome her. Cherubs singing, their mouths pink and plump, their cheeks velvety, their eyes damp with joy. They were barefoot and wore gold crowns and silk tunics bound to their chests with cords that were also golden. And amid the angels was Our Lord. Our Lord, who had a face like Francesc's, with a dimple in the middle of His chin. His rough hands, covered in rings, grasped her face to kiss her as her husband had kissed her on their wedding day. *Welcome to my Eternal Glory*, He would say to her. And then, when amid the joyous, gleaming light Margarida again saw the Lord's mouth before hers, the Lord's eyes like two gleaming spoons, His gaze so close upon her that He could see every single thing that poor woman had had to bear, He cried tears that looked like milk.

But alas!, my girls, what a disappointment. Because when Margarida died, hands clasped, her fingernails first pink, then white, her mouth open, and her snowy eyes fixed on everlasting joy, every bit of her was prepared—panting, desirous, and whipped—yet there were no cherubs, no trumpets; there was no luminous flare, no spasm of glory, no conclusive joy, no smothering ecstasy. Just a circle of dirty, surly women. Grotesque and ordinary. That's right. As sad as it sounds. Because when Margarida's little three-quarters heart finally cried enough!, when it failed, knotted up, that's all, folks, fare thee well!, her relatives encircled her. And instead of heaven and the angels and God's hands wiping her cheeks, she was surrounded by her mother, Joana, like a toothless mare, her sister Blanca, who was the only one she was at all happy to see and even then not so much, her niece, Àngela, who in death still looked like a wild boar, and Elisabet. Had Margarida not been so stunned and diminished, she would've ripped every last hair out of Elisabet's head. But they were dead! All four of them. Holy Mother of God, some of them had been dead for many years. Souls sent to damnation! Margarida twisted and turned, unable to say a word, so terrified and bewildered was she. Nobody would've heard her anyway, because her relatives were all screaming, *Margarida, Margarida, MARGARIDA!* as they lifted her up by the armpits and cackled, and her mother was smiling at her with holes where her teeth should have been and saying, *Welcome, Margarida, welcome back!*, as if the devil himself had opened up the gates of hell for her. Poor Margarida, still warm, looked at them with eyes narrowed to the size of pine nuts, as terrifying as her relatives were, horrific!, even uglier than she'd remembered, and she thought she must be dreaming, this couldn't be, she hadn't died, not yet, not that, impossible, no, no, no, please, Lord, please, for the love of God, for the Virgin and all the saints and all the angels.

If it were up to Margarida, when old Bernadeta died, because it couldn't be long now, there would be no festivities. The only thing her useless relatives thought about and talked about lately—on and on they'd go about silverware, about the nursling goat, about the glasses with blue stems, about the fritters and the gravy stew—was the party, the party, the party, every single thing was about the godforsaken party. Joana would sit in the kitchen, presiding from her bench and giving orders, over here, over there, do that and do this, and the women wandered through the house, conspiring. If Margarida had her way, when that old woman died, they would organize a sober welcome, austere, respectful, and serene. Not like the one she'd had.

How she'd cried. How poor Margarida had cried when, instead of rising up to heaven to be received by the shepherd of souls, she was dragged downstairs by the ghastly, insufferable women of her house, who were always sticking their fingers in wounds. They dragged her, when they could've just rolled her down. They lugged her to the kitchen and they sat her at the table set with plates, cups, and bowls. And then they opened their mouths and drank and ate and howled and clapped and made toasts and celebrated and sat up and straightened their necks and lifted their arms into the air. The repulsive dish they placed before Margarida filled with tears. Like a soup. But not a single one of her relatives was able to console her. Not a single one tried. Not her mother. Who'd ripped her from her entrails. All her mother did was fribble away the time, shouting and drinking and telling jokes and pounding her cup against the table. Joana was pure uproar and revelry, there on her bench, her place at the table. Margarida watched her in terror. The others shrieked and egged her on. She was dancing! As if she had no memory, or as if she wanted to obliterate it. As if she didn't remember the things she didn't want to remember. As if in that gruesome kitchen, filled with ghosts, she no longer cared about the things of the past. Entire lives. Daughters and mothers.

The house creaked as if cracking its knuckles. Then there was a long silence, broken by the owl outside, followed by more silence. The night curled up inside the farmhouse like a small beast, and shadows moseyed through, footless. Each corner had its own deep, heavy, cavernous blackness. The room where Bernadeta slept was doleful. The sitting room was lugubrious. The stairs were like a well. The entrance was sinister. The kitchen was a wolf's throat. Bottomless. The walls, the hearth, the window, the table, the chairs, and the sink couldn't be seen. As if they weren't there. As if there were no kitchen, no house. Just dusk and gloom. Joana was sitting on her bench. She was very old. She had a horse face, one eye opened wider than the other, her shambolic gray hair like a mane, her arms thick and her belly wide. That was her spot. The bench beside the fireplace, even though the fire was never lit anymore.

Joana had married the heir to Mas Clavell in Sant Miquel dels Barretons long ago, more years ago than anyone could count. The ceremony was simple, austere, and took place at midmorning, so the newlyweds would have time to get back to the house before nightfall. Husband and wife climbed along rugged paths and craggy slopes featuring every shade of green. They crossed mountain ranges, hills, canyons, gullies, and lush, moist ravines among beeches and aspens, birches and almond trees, holm oaks, elms, and chorleywood bushes that grew denser in a stifling embrace until light fell upon the newlyweds' clothes like a handful of spare coins. Joana and Bernadí spent an entire day making their way through those secluded and snarled mountains, stopping only whenever they came upon a wayside shrine. Bernadí would lower his head, close his eyes, and ask the Lord to keep his path clear of wolves and evildoers. Joana would be beside him with her palms pressed together, but she didn't pray. She was watching him. They were already married, but they'd met only three days earlier, and she had scarcely had a moment to look at him. She studied his purple hands, covered in calluses, his fingers like fat sausages, his hairy nape, his oversize back, his nose like a turnip, his forehead full of rolls of fat, and his thick beard, which climbed his cheeks like brambles all the way up to his eyebrows. But Bernadí's prayers were in vain, and Joana barely had time to conclude that her husband looked like a hog, because not long after midday, those evil beasts began their howling. It froze the blood in your veins. Each howl was like a cold dagger dragged down your back and to your belly; if you didn't breathe, it wouldn't pierce you, it would just roil the contents of your stomach. And Bernadí, who had sensed the beasts for a while now, anxiously surveying the greenness and the blueness between the trees and the sudden movements of the branches, cursed and spat. He walked, leading the way, and Joana watched. She was rattled to see him kicking at rocks and trees, and then, without slowing his hurried pace, he turned his left foot inward as if it weren't his and brutishly dragged it across the ground. They hadn't taken even a hundred steep steps after the howling had begun, when, grinding his teeth, Bernadí threw himself onto his knees beneath a wild thicket, and from his espadrille freed a gray foot with thick yellow nails, then frantically scratched and scratched and scratched. And that was when she saw it. Saint Lucy! Holy Mother of God! Bernadí's stinky, hairy foot had only four toes. Only four toes! Joana's heart nearly leaped out through her mouth, such was her joy. She could hardly resist the urge to kneel down beside him and cover that trotter with kisses, like Mary Magdalene. But then Bernadí grew calm. He slipped his reddened, inflamed foot back into his espadrille, and man and woman continued walking, the dusk and the shrieks of the beasts nipping at their heels. Before they reached

Mas Clavell, Bernadí, taciturn and pragmatic, said they'd been five siblings in that house, but the other four had been carried off by wolves. First they'd eaten the sheep. When there were no more sheep, they snuck into the house and devoured his siblings whole, but for one arm and a piece of his sister's head. Yet Bernadí, the eldest, had twisted and thrashed maniacally, screeching like a soul damned to hell, and he wasn't eaten by the wild beasts. He'd seemed to them like too much work. They'd managed only to tear off his left pinkie toe in a single clumsy bite. And now, instead of a pinkie toe, his foot had a bumpy, shiny white scar that itched like hell when he heard them howling.

Bernadí's mother had fallen ill. After the wolves devoured four of her children as if they were chickens, she'd swelled up. First her feet, purple. Then her knees, black. Then her belly, like a bird fallen from the nest. And she died. Then the beasts, as if they understood affronts and grudges, dug up her grave and ate her face and hands. Bernadí and his father, having been left alone together, exclaimed, That's it! That's the final straw! And they started a war. They placed themselves in the hands of the Holy Spirit Our Defender, Saint Blaise the Glorious, Saint Paul, Saint Agatha, and Saint Anthony, keep us safe from evil and the devil, the wolf and the hound and the beasts who confound, and they set out to find dens. Which are always southward facing and near water. They schemed about how to destroy litters that nurse until they're twenty-five days old. And about how to make rope snares and trick planks. They placed some bait on the far end of a board hanging over a cliff. The plank was held in place by a rock covered with branches. And when the animal climbed out onto it to fetch the food, it would fall off the cliff. They bound arrow points two by two with horsehair. They tied six or seven in a row, turned them in alternating directions, and when they were well spiky, they inserted them into a piece of meat, bigger than the arrow points but small enough to be gulped down in one bite. They left a bit of gristly meat here, a bit there, and the wolves swallowed the bait without chewing. When they digested it, the arrows would open into the shape of a cross and puncture their guts.

During the good years, in the township of Dosrius, father and son killed wolves eight by eight. In Vilamajor, seven by seven. Near Sant Hilari, by the half dozen. In Espinelves and Viladrau, they trapped the biggest she-wolves; beneath Les Agudes mountains, the largest litters; and in Sant Sadurní d'Osormort, and in Sant Celoni, and in Vilanova de Sau and Rupit and Folgueroles, they killed so many they lost count. Bernadí and his father located the beasts and warned the families in the concerned houses, who gathered up the nearby folk. When given the sign by Bernadí's father, the master wolfhunter, they shouted and clanged chains to tighten the scope of the drive and lead the wolves down narrow tracks, toward the trapping pits and to the cliffs where they would fall to their death. Where they were killed with rocks, pikes, hand slings, javelins, and wolf gibbets, where they were flayed end to end, or left for the dogs to tear apart. Bernadí's father enjoyed the drives. For the company, for the men's shouts and laughter, and for the wolves' terror and howling at the mob. But one day, near Seva, a cornered beast pounced on the old man and bit his face in such a way that even when they'd managed to kill the wolf, its snout was still clamped on the man's mouth. As if they were kissing. Bernadí's father was left with a maimed jaw and holes in his cheeks, and he could scarcely swallow, although soon that wouldn't matter. Because that she-wolf was rabid. And rabies makes you detest food and water. First he complained of headaches. Later the muscles of his face began to move of their own accord, and you could see his teeth through the holes in his cheeks. Then the writhing began. After that he turned furious. Foamed at the nose and mouth. And Bernadí thought, horrified, that if those treacherous beasts had trapped him, too, if they'd attacked him from behind and eaten him in some cave, then they would have won the battle. He put an end to his father's suffering and rushed to the nearest town, which was Seva, to find a woman to marry.

Joana perspired and panted as she tried to match the vigorous strides of her groom, thinking how she'd awaited him for so long! For she had, indeed. Oh, how she'd waited for him! Because Joana had asked for a man in every possible way one can ask for a man. To no avail. She had asked God and the Virgin and Saint Anthony, but they didn't listen to her. Until one day Garreta—an old woman who toiled with her in Seva, who ate only bread soup with milk, because she lacked even a single tooth, and Joana would look at her and think, Good Lord, please don't let me be like Garreta, alone and old and toothless, eating bread soup with milk—asked her, *Why are you crying, dearie?* Joana replied that she was crying because she had the face of a horse. The face of a mare. And saying it made her cry even harder, because God and the Virgin and Saint Anthony had turned their backs on her and left her to bolt like lettuce, with no suitor who wanted her. But Garreta tempted her: *If One doesn't listen, why not ask it of the Other?* Joana replied in a thin wisp of a voice that she didn't know how to ask something of the Other. Garreta offered her help. She said that if Joana wanted, she could explain it to her. She said that if she was asking for only one thing, it was best to go alone, at daybreak. That she had to kill a cat. Not too small and not too big. Medium-sized. And stick a fava bean in each of its eyes, a fava in its mouth, and a fava in its asshole. And that she had to bury it, and on the mound she had to draw a cross, and on the cross she had to piss. Then the devil would come and she could ask for what she needed.

Joana saw him as she was shaking the piss off her legs. Amid the trees. First his eyes. Because they sparkled. Then the blotch that was his thick neck and hump and back. Then the rest of the bull. Because he was a bull. Magnificent. All black, like the blackest thing. His horns were black; the flesh inside his eyes was black; black were his eyelashes; black were his ears; black was his snout, filled with snot, his forehead covered in cowlicks, his veiny neck, his legs, his hooves, his belly, his backside, his pudenda: black. So dark that the night seemed pale. And he approached. His fur gleamed as if it were water. Hot vapor poured from his nostrils, and he stank, as if the water were dirty and stagnant. It was a living stink, piercing. Joana let her skirt drop and stood up. The bull asked, in a sweeter and more wistful voice than she could ever have imagined, *What dost thou want, Sovereign Mistress?* Joana replied like a little bird singing, *I want a full man*, she said, *a man of my own, an heir with a patch of land and a roof over his head.* The devil accepted the terms. Joana's soul in exchange for a husband. Then he left beneath a sliver of moon in search of a cow. The next day, Bernadí Clavell asked for Joana's hand.

Bernadí preferred cleverness to brute force. Stealthy silence. Solitude. After his father died, he'd hunted the wolves alone, using snares and traps with arms of nails and spikes that snapped shut. He would dip them in manure juice so the wily beasts wouldn't smell the scent of iron and of men. And he followed trails and searched out turds. The mountains were full of big piles of turds. Stone martens would shit on the roads haphazardly: the females, thin little poops; the males, thick ones. Genets would lay their loads on craggy rocks, making piles, always in the same places. Badgers would dig latrines. Foxes shat wherever they wanted. If he caught any of those creatures, he would kill them too. Delicately. He would place his foot on their neck, squeeze their ribs, and choke them. The genets and the stone martens died quickly, without a fight. The badgers and the foxes required more patience, waiting a good long while before they suffocated. Once they were dead, he would pull their bones, flesh, and innards out through their mouths, without tearing the skin. He would fill the hides with forest hay until they were taut and wrinkle-free, and then, when he went down into the towns, he'd sell them.

There was no need for delicacy when it came to killing wolves. They shat everywhere. Out in the open. Like a sign. At crossroads, on cliffs. So you would see it. So you would have to acknowledge them. Those damn bastards knew precisely how to attack each living thing: sheep by the neck, pigs by the belly, cows by the udder to make them kneel, horses and donkeys any way they could—because those back legs really kicked—and it was best to grab the young ones. Children by the head. And if they found an animal who'd just given birth, they knew they had to yank on the placenta and the cord, to wound them on the inside. If they'd just had a kill, they shat soft, dark liquid, because the first thing they ate was the blood and entrails, which dyed their shit black, and if they had been picking at the carcass, they produced dry, hairy, white piles of dung. They were the demons of those mountains, and Bernadí killed them without a second thought.

For a wolf or a she-wolf, they would give him a silver coin worth five sous. For a litter, five more. And after paying him, they would give him a certificate with a seal, so he could go off happily and pass the hat in the villages. *Here you have the traitor who emptied your corrals. This is the nasty beast who did so much harm and tore out the throats of your flocks. All those who want to give, give.* People would offer him round cakes and dried fruit and nuts, and

Bernadí would return to Mas Clavell with his hands covered in nicks and cuts, a bag full of silver coins and another filled with sweets. He sat down at the table, famished, as if he hadn't eaten the whole time he'd been gone, and he devoured the victuals Joana placed before him, roaring with gratitude, his face right up close to the plate and his eyes misty with the steam. Broth from the hearty soup dripped from his beard and fingers and elbows, and when he'd finished, he hugged his wife with greasy hands, like someone newly fortified. And Joana, beneath that pine tree of a man, uncovered a fly agaric like no other. A toadstool, the size of her hand, that she stroked delicately, careful not to break its buttery stalk. Because Bernadí was ugly as a wart, Joana could admit that, but oh, what a sweet toadstool he had! Holy Mother of God, what a toadstool. Velvety and hard and pretty as all get-out. Red and white and shiny with dew. As if he were hiding all his delicacy, all his beauty, all his joy down there below in the form of a hat, ring, spores, and stalk, rooted in the dark earth. Toadstool, toadstool, who planted you there? The Holy Virgin with her five fingers, amid the maidenhair!

The second time, the devil showed up in the guise of a man. One hooded night he went to the farmhouse to collect on the debt. But Joana loved that house so very much, like a snail loves its shell, like a soul loves its body, that it was as if she were gazing out at him from within armor, from behind a fortress wall. He was an ugly, haggard, bald man, with a white face and a huge mouth. And he stank as much as the bull, but now, in the stench, Joana could also make out traces of goat, asscrack, and bonfires. She did not invite him in. The demon greeted her with a voice both measured and pompous: *Good evening, Sovereign Mistress.* She did not respond in kind. She blurted out, *Bernadí is not a full man.* But it seemed that the evil beast did not understand, and

Joana had to explain it to him: *I asked for a* full *man, who owned a patch of land and had a roof over his head, but Bernadí is not a full man.* The Great Spit-Roaster looked at her incredulously. Joana added, *He's missing his left pinkie toe.* At that, there followed a clamor and a terrible crack, and then it rained cats and dogs for four days straight. The heavy downpour made the bridges of Sau, Querós, Sallent, and Susqueda crumble.

Joana put the devil out of her mind, convinced she'd gotten the best of him, until her eldest daughter was born. Margarida. A slender baby with a severe and reproving gaze, and a frenetic, frightened blue chest. Joana put an ear to her ribs and shuddered. Because even though it wasn't visible, if you listened you could hear it: There was something wrong with the baby girl's heart. It was missing a piece. Which didn't mean that Margarida had a bad heart. No. Or a delicate heart. Not that either. It meant her heart was small, tough, stringy. Hard to chew. Rancorous. The size of a hare's. After Margarida, Joana gave birth to Blanca, who was born without a tongue. Her mouth like an empty nest. And Joana again felt a prickle of suspicion, but she didn't put it all together. Then came Esperança. Her poor little Esperança, who was born without a liver and died yellow as a little chick. And it felt impossible, leaving that bundle all alone, at night and secretly, in a cold, dark hole in the ground, near the wall of Sant Miquel dels Barretons, so she would be close to God. But Joana still didn't want to believe it. And then came her firstborn son. Whom she would have named Bernadí, like his father, if not for the fact that he was born without a hole back there and died, stuffed like a sausage. His flesh hard and purple. And as Bernadí carried that second bundle to Sant Miquel, Joana understood. She got it. She saw that everything has a price. And that the price is too high, every time. And that after the pact she'd made with the devil, and then unmade, thanks to her husband's missing pinkie toe, all her progeny would be missing something. She looked at her house, her man, her severe daughter, her mute daughter, and she thought how it was still much more than Garreta had. And by dint of willow, ivy, almond tree root, pennyroyal, and hemp, she quelled that flow of defective babies.

Bernadeta offered up deep, raspy snores that resounded in isolation. The walls resisted them and then, right after, swallowed them up. Every once in a while, the rhythm was interrupted when she turned in her bed, sighed, and smacked her lips. Her bald eyelids trembled. Margarida sat by her side and prayed with increasing vehemence, because it is in the blackest heart of the night, in the dark hour just before the break of dawn, that the devil and his envoys camp at their leisure. It had been a sticky dawn when the demon had tempted her mother. It had been a poisonous dawn when Joana had confessed to Margarida her unforgivable sin. The woman had shrieked, *Bernadí! What have they done to you? Bernadí, my sweet toadstool!*, and Margarida, who was still a naive young girl, had consoled her. Joana looked like a grieving Holy Virgin, with her tears streaming and her head falling forward, as if her neck had grown tired of holding it up. It had been three nights since she'd slept a wink, because Margarida's father had not returned, and he would not return, and as soon as Joana shut her lids, she would imagine them, treacherous wolves tearing him apart: *Bernadí!* Wicked bandits slicing into his double chin like they were sharing a round bread: *Bernadí!* Soft crags swallowing him and filling his ears with mud and dirty water, as if they were stuffing him: *Bernadí! Bernadí!* Margarida said, *Sssh, Mother, sssh*, and Joana shouted, *My toadstool, my sweet toadstool. I know he's dead, I know it, he's dead, because I've become an old woman suddenly and without warning!* she bellowed. And then she entered the memories as if going into a forest. But she didn't pass into that perfidious thicket alone. No. She took one of Margarida's hands and pulled the poor girl in with her beneath the trees. She took her along the very same paths that Joana and Bernadí had traveled after marrying. Margarida listened innocently, and every so often repeated, *Sssh, Mother, sssh*, to comfort her. But all of a sudden the forest surrounding them changed. It became dense and ominous, and Margarida wanted to go home. She did not want to continue down that path. She did not want to draw closer to the clearing Joana was pointing to. Her mother forced her. She gripped her and even scratched her. And within the darkness Margarida could see a white butt, from behind, pissing. She yelped when she realized it was Joana's butt. Then a black bull appeared and approached her mother. Joana whispered into her ear, *the devil*, but Margarida shook her head like a chicken that's just been plucked. She wasn't listening. No. She didn't hear her. She put her hands over her ears, NA-NA-NA. But Joana, whose eyes were empty like almond shells and whose teeth were sparse and pointy, yanked them away. All Margarida wanted, please, she was begging, was for Joana to shut up. So she could forget about that bull and ignore the pact he'd made with her mother. She didn't want to know anything about her three-quarters heart, or Blanca's tongue, or Esperança's liver, or the heir's bunghole. The poor girl clung to the kitchen table and thought about her father. Bernadí, who was good, who smelled acidic and smoky, of dried blood and sweat, when he sat his two girls on his lap and taught them the prayer of protection from the wolf. Or told them about the things God had done and the things the devil had done. He would tell them, *God made the trees and the rivers and the mountains and the pretty and useful animals. And the devil made the ugly wild animals.* And Margarida imagined it, seated on his lap. How

God made the goldfinch, and made the swallow, and made the nightingale. And how the devil, to sully the world, made the bat, and the owl, and the raven. *God made the cat, and the devil made the rat. God made the horse, and the devil, the snake. God made the sheep, and the devil, the goat.* But Joana stuck a prickly tongue into Margarida's ear and shook her as if she'd wanted to snatch her off her father's lap. God made the pear tree, and the apple tree, and the chestnut tree, and the Virginia creeper, and the Scotch broom, and the rosebush, and the devil made the hawthorn, the buckeye, the blackberry bush, the gorse, the dog rose, and the common rue. God made wheat, and the devil, wild oats. God made the bee, and the devil, the wasp. God made the ladybug, and the devil, the cockroach. God made the eagle, the turtledove, the chaffinch, the blackbird, and the skylark, and the devil made the carrion crow, the jay, the sparrow, the thrush, and the hawk. And when, in spite of all that, God was still winning, the devil made the wolf, to have the last word. Their father always told them, with Margarida on one leg, Blanca on the other, that they should never, never, never leave the house alone. Because in the big piles of shit left by the animals he hunted, he would find small clothes and small bones that belonged to kids. In Osor, since he'd been keeping track, the wolves had eaten eight children. They'd devoured seven from Susqueda. In a single farmhouse near Tavertet, they'd killed two and wounded two more. Two at a house near Viladrau. Three toddlers and a baby girl in a crib in Sant Sadurní d'Osormort; two girls and their mother in Campins; three kids, a doctor, and a mule in Sant Feliu de Buixalleu.

By the time Joana's venomous gushing had finally dried up, daylight was spilling through the window. And Margarida suddenly realized, when she saw the table, the chairs, the cold fireplace, her mother's hands—her face wrinkled, her eyes cold, her mouth stubborn—that for the first time she found her old. Ugly. Treacherous. Then they heard the shouting. On the threshing floor. *Hail Mary!* they cried out. *Hail Mary!* And mother and daughter sat up, but they didn't have time to comb their hair or dry their cheeks before a man entered the house, like morning does, without knocking. He crossed the threshold and went into the kitchen. He gave a slight bow and said, *Ladies.* Flustered, Margarida looked at him and thought, He must be a prince. Or an angel. Only eyes that had witnessed heaven's glory could've alighted on such a man. Her heart and her frozen limbs came back to life because she was imagining how Our Lord had made him. On the same day He'd made little goldfinches and swallows. Of the best clay. Of the clay He used to make the pretty, useful animals. With His hands. And she saw it, how He had modeled that mouth, in the spot where the mouth goes, and inside He had placed the teeth, one by one, and how He made the dimple in the middle of his chin, and his eyes, like two torches. How He had sculpted that colt's neck, his chest and back, his legs with their round knees. How He had chiseled his fingers, which held the small cup Joana offered him, without drinking from it. And how He'd placed a nail at each tip, like a gem. His lips spoke. His name was Francesc Llobera. He explained that he was the younger son of a house called Mas Llobera, near Viladrau, where the women were dropping like flies, and he wanted to leave. So that he wouldn't die of tedium along with them, after watching his father and elder brother marry again and again. When he smiled, his lips stretched. He glanced around the kitchen, at the walls, the ceiling, the widow, the heiress. Joana said, *Margarida is good, healthy, and hardworking.* Francesc asked, *Do you have any other daughters?* Joana replied, *Yes, but Blanca is a simpleton.* Because Blanca watched the hens. How they pecked at the ground, distracted.

And the rooster, how he lifted one leg, and how he lifted the other leg. And how he puffed up his chest and crowed. He moved his wings, which were too short to fly. He turned his neck and scratched himself. He crowed some more and ruffled his feathers. His crest and wattles jiggled. The hen crouched down, obliging, and the rooster climbed atop. He mounted her back with his legs, he grabbed her neck feathers in his beak, and they shook.

And then Joana said, If Francesc and Margarida were to marry, and at these words Margarida's three-quarters heart began to flip-flop as Joana paused before repeating, if Francesc and her daughter were to marry, and Margarida thought, God must love her so very much if He was giving her that man to wed!, but then Joana went on to declare that if Francesc and her daughter were to marry, they would have to support and shelter, for the rest of their natural lives, mother-in-law and mother, respectively—i.e., herself—and, sister-in-law and sister respectively—i.e., Blanca—in sickness and in health, and provide them with food and drink and shoes and clothes, and when they slipped into oblivion, they would have to bury them. And Francesc looked at Margarida, who sat very still, silent, her heart still flip-flopping, her head lowered, and her hands in her lap, and he chose her. Among all the girls from whom to choose, from the whole string of women across the world, with their eyes and their hair and their gazes, he said, This one. And he pointed to her.

They made a meal of turnips in walnut sauce. They washed the turnips, they cut them, they boiled them twice over. They strained them, and in a pan they sautéed an onion with lard, and when the onion was cooked, they set it aside. They sprinkled flour in the remaining fat, and when it turned blond they added the turnips. They made the sauce separately. With walnuts, milk, the sautéed onion, and wine. And they cooked pigeons in brown sauce. They plucked them and took out their livers, which they chopped with bread dipped in wine and vinegar. They boiled three eggs, removed the yolks, and mixed them with the bread and the livers, and then they strained the mixture and put it into a pot and boiled it in honey. They roasted the pigeons, and when they were half-cooked, they put them into the pot with the liver sauce. And they made apples in apple gravy. With the sweetest fruit—peeled, chopped, and cored—which they boiled in water. And separately they prepared the sauce with a handful of toasted almonds they crushed in a mortar and drowned in the apple broth to make almond milk, to which they added soft bread and honey.

The parson of Querós posted the marriage banns. No one had any objections, and the bride and groom were married in the presence of their relatives. The parson said the marriage rites. *Thee, Francesc Llobera, do offer your body to Margarida as she stands before thee, as a loyal husband. Dixit quod sic. Et eodem modo dixit. Thee, Margarida Clavell, do offer your body as loyal wife to Llobera as he stands before thee. Que nullum dedit responsum.* And Francesc, with the dimple in the middle of his chin and his rough hands covered in rings, held her cheeks, and the joy was so brilliant that Margarida couldn't see a thing.

Then the bells rang. Bells upon bells. Pealing. Shrill and metallic. Bells inside the house. Bells that weren't celebrating nuptials, but ringing out the dead; forewarning of fire, of wolves, of storms, of thieves, they cautioned against the terrible things that were already drawing near, so that everyone would awaken. And the parlor was filled with light. Like a slap across the face. It was a dirty light. Mendacious. Yellow. An outrage. The false gleam slipped in under the door, and Margarida, who was sitting in the dark beside Bernadeta, twiddling her thumbs, jumped up from her chair, as if she'd sat on a pin. Weasel footsteps were heard approaching. The doorknob turned with a faint groan. And even though the trees and the forest outside refused to renounce the darkness, clinging to the shadows, to the dampness and the crunching, the artificial light contradicting them won out and suffocateded the blackness like a flood. Marta entered the room. She was an ugly woman, in Margarida's view, podgy, with a round face, generous shoulders, a prominent bosom, and a copious bum. Her hair was messy and plastered to her skull, and she wore a shabby nightgown of two pink pieces covered in rabbits with gray bellies and white ears. Around her neck hung tortoiseshell spectacles, and in her hand she carried a little mirror. And the entire church was there, inside the little mirror. And inside the church were the bells, pealing. On the bedside table, Marta lit a second accursed false light, a light without flame, that wouldn't go out if you blew on it. Only if you hit it. But you had to hit it hard. Bam! Bam! Bam! Margarida hit them when no one was looking. And then, when Marta tried to light them and the witchcraft failed to work, Marta grumbled, unbelievable!, the wiring in this house is total crap!

Marta murmured Bernadeta's name, and Margarida turned away because that light was fallacious and annoying, and because she didn't want to see Marta or what she was doing. Marta was alive. There was a vexing path she had not traveled. Not yet. She'd been born, like all things that are born. But Marta hadn't died. Not yet. Like all things that die. And it was divine law, universal law, fundamental law—no matter how many times the women of that house pissed on the fundamental laws—that you didn't look at the living, or touch them, or speak to them. Zero contact. Turn your back. Ignore them! Like you would a toad, or a stinging nettle, or a cow patty. Bernadeta moved her lips, she clapped her tongue inside her woolly mouth, she swallowed saliva and opened two lashless eyes, like two wounds. Marta said good morning, and the old woman made a sound that to Margarida seemed tepid. She asked her if she wanted to make pee-pee, and, without waiting for her to answer, she pulled off the sheets and blankets. Bernadeta was wearing a threadbare nightgown that revealed her transparent arms with their long flaps. She lowered her bare legs from the bed, shoved her beefy feet into some espadrilles, and ran one arm over Marta's shoulders. And slowly, gradually, because she was an irksome old lady, she stood up and they departed the room, leaving the lamp lit. Margarida snorted. The insolence! As if now women and men could choose when it was day and when it was night. They strolled through the world as if they owned it, as if they had the right to see everything, even that which shouldn't be seen. So brazen! As if it were no longer God who had the measure of all things, and no longer He who chose the darkness of the nights and the length of the days. She heard them crossing the parlor. Going into the outhouse that they'd shamelessly built indoors, and Bernadeta's rump making a cold slap as it fell onto the toilet. It was of white porcelain, as if they were duchesses. And she heard the sound of the cow's stream. And Marta's voice asked Bernadeta if she'd slept well. More indifferent sounds from the old lady. If she was hungry, and Bernadeta mumbled, mmmh, if she wanted to go downstairs for breakfast, which was the only question the old woman answered clearly. No. Then they were back in the room, draggling, and they sat down on the bed, which was high, short, austere, with a headboard of metal bars. Marta opened a bottle that couldn't break, and she poured water into a green cup of good glass. On the night table there was a mountain of boxes, white, blue, gray, that Marta rummaged through. The old woman held out a trembling hand, and Marta placed seeds in it. A red one. A blue-and-orange one. Two small white ones. A round one with a line down the middle. Bernadeta gulped them down. Marta refilled the cup and then tossed in a yellow coin, which moved inside the water like someone drowning, sputtering out bubbles. When it was engulfed, Bernadeta drank it, and Marta told her that she would bring her up some toast and chamomile tea for breakfast. The old woman asked for jam, and Marta left, closing the door and leaving the false light on the bedside table lit. As if all the others weren't punishment and disgrace enough!, thought Margarida. All the churlish, ghastly, weak, lazy, insidious, sticking-fingers-in-wounds women of that house. On top of all that, she had to put up with Marta, who was coarse, thick, a misbegotten pudden-headed ass. But that wasn't all Margarida'd been condemned to. Oh no. Because her suffering knew no end. Marta had a daughter called Alexandra. Fruit of sin and vice, like most of the spawn of that house. And Alexandra hadn't even been born in the house. She'd been born outside. That was why the scalawag was a rootless, slippery backslider without a care in the world, and she hardly ever spent the night there. And an unbelieving woman might have thought it a fortunate thing that Marta's lazy daughter, who had no patience, no drive, no blood in her veins, and not a smidgen of respect, hardly ever slept at Mas Clavell. But who knows where she slept! As if no one had ever learned their lesson in that house. Tripping over the same stones time and again. Alexandra was sleeping with men, and with demons! While her mother, Marta, who was as dumb as the day is long, a tormentor, an oblivious know-nothing, who knew so little she didn't even know who Margarida was!, sauntered through the house as if it were hers, turning lights on and off and pissing in corners, scatterbrained and completely empty-headed, her head so empty it went cling-cling, clang-clang, clong-clong.

MORNING

> . . . for women live much more in the past
> than we do, he thought, they attach themselves
> to places . . .
>
> VIRGINIA WOOLF, *MRS. DALLOWAY*

The kitchen window was narrow and deep like an ear canal. An oblique, early, bluish light slipped through it, muting shapes and colors. The peeling walls and the chimney hood were white, the damp patches were gray, the counter was yellow, the sink joints were black, the cupboards were in brown tones with metal pulls dotted with rust, the floor was of burgundy tile, the benches, chairs, and table were of pinewood with varying patinas of wear and varnish. The kitchen had two doors. A solid one, with two steps in front that led to a pantry as purple and cold as a liver. And another with glass panels that opened onto the entryway. The farmhouse's entrance was damp and dark, like a throat. With rough walls, which were the fleshy insides of the cheeks. With a beamed ceiling like a striped palate, and a rock floor, which was a tongue worn down by countless years of swallowing. There was a rack filled with shoes placed any which way. A bench. A small built-in cupboard with worm-eaten doors and a wooden latch. Three hooks covered with jackets, like hunched backs. A box filled with empty glass bottles. On the walls hung cheese-making tools: a slicer and basket molds. On the ground were two milk cans, just for show. The arch of the doorway was the gums. The closed door that led outside, gritted teeth. Tiled stairs, narrow as a backbone, led to the upper floor. The depths of the throat that was the entrance opened onto long sties of pressed earth, with a single window, walls with built-in feeders along them, a rudimentary sink, sacks, pails, a pitchfork, fodder and hay, metal shelving that held tools and dust, and a way out that opened onto a corral. The sties were divided in two. On one side there were four lanky goats. On the other, a festive coach. One of the goats was white. Another was brown. The buck was black. And there was a kid that was brown with a white face. The coach was gold and blue, and had cushions and embroidered edging, fringes made of folded silk, and painted gold stars.

Marta entered the kitchen, and Joana, from her bench, watched as she disappeared into the pantry and reemerged with two slices of bread, milk, jam, and butter. Marta toasted the bread over embers that never blew out, grabbed a mug, filled it with milk, and placed it inside the glass urn that sat on the counter. The urn lit up and hummed. The mug spun round and round. Standing, Marta placed onto her nose the fingerprint-covered spectacles that hung around her neck and looked at her little mirror. She stroked it with her thumb. Quickly, quickly. She scrutinized it, and her finger went up and up. And then stopped. She looked into it some more, and then she laughed suddenly at the things the little mirror showed her. Marta's laughter infected Joana with a crooked smile. The old woman slapped her knees. *When women laugh and donkeys bray, that there's the devil having his say.* And then Joana really let loose. Her eyes dampened, her buckled smile turned sarcastic and cunning, and the old woman burst out laughing, braying like an ass, and her amusement was so raucous she nearly choked on it. A high-pitched little bell rang and the light in the urn went out. Marta opened its little glass door and pulled out the steaming mug. She tossed in a spoonful of dark powder and the milk turned black. With a knife, she took curls of butter and placed them atop one of the slices of bread. Hardly bothering to spread it, she nibbled, and while still eating she filled a second mug with water from the swan's mouth, placed it inside the urn, and spread jam on the other slice. Joana snorted three times with her mouth open and then settled down.

When Francesc Llobera married Margarida and moved to Mas Clavell, he brought a valet with him named Bou, which means "steer." *One woman, fine. Two women, plenty. Three women, too much.* The valet's upper lip was stuck to his nose, and his eyelashes, brows, beard, hair, and even all the hairs inside his nose were so blond that he looked more like a sheep than a steer. He loved his master's proverbs. *When a woman is hairy, even the devil is wary. When the devil can't make it, he sends a woman in his stead. When the devil is full of doubt, he asks a woman. Where women are not, the devil, he will bring them.* Bou would nod in agreement. *When the devil wants to learn, to women he will turn. Once, the devil gambled with a woman and she won.* At night, Francesc would bid them, *Kneel. Pray. Repent.* And the women and Bou would kneel down. They would lower their heads and listen as the man lectured them about how nothing grew the way it should grow in that house or on those dry, barren, bewitched lands that surrounded it. Such was the curse that hovered over that house, he would exclaim, that when plants sprouted there, they sprouted for Satan, and onto whatsoever Jesus planted, the Fallen One would place his graft, and all that was intended for God there in Mas Clavell bore fruits for the devil! Until one morning Bou said, *Ye needn't worry henceforth, ladies, for we have killed the witch. Which witch?* asked Joana and Margarida. Bou replied, *The old one in Pou de Querós.* And they knew which woman he was speaking of. Segimona Vila, who had one wild eye and a crippled daughter. According to the valet, the demon and the old woman chained up the girl each night and mounted her as if she were a mule. And he explained that his master had given him a gold doubloon for going to the neighboring house and shooting the sorceress right in the forehead with his blunderbuss. When Bou found old Segimona Vila folding a tablecloth, he commanded, *Get thee hither, and touch me not! For that is what ye witches do, always wanting to touch.* Old Vila went to the corner the valet pointed to, and the man aimed his gun between her two eyes, between the one that went this way and the one that went that, as he said, *This is the castigation for having bewitched the fields of Mas Clavell, and for having killed our two pigs. Ye needn't worry henceforth, ladies; our misfortune has ended,* he repeated, and proudly added that with a knife he had separated the tendons on her heels and below her knees so that after the witch's burial, her evil spirit couldn't rise.

The little bell on the urn sounded again, and Marta sank a small sachet of herbs into the mug of water. She took one last bite of the bread and butter, a last sip of the black milk, licked the knife, put the little mirror into her pocket, placed her spectacles on her head like a tiara, then picked up Bernadeta's breakfast and left. And Joana revived and stood up. She placed a bony hand, with fingers that twisted in all four directions, onto the table, and she left her bench, dragging her feet. Her ankles were thick, her knees swollen, and her back twisted.

When Margarida's first child was due, Joana and Blanca covered the windows and sealed the doors so that no drafts or wicked things could enter. They set to boil an infusion of laurel, wormwood, and yellow iris. Joana repeated, *I beseech thee, child, whether male or female, in the name of the Father and the Son and the Holy Ghost, to go forward and not backward and not to hurt your mother.* It was the long labor of a first-time mother. When the baby was out, they inspected him carefully. Finger by finger. They felt his belly, his little legs, his private parts, his back covered in velvet, but they couldn't find anything missing. Margarida cried with relief. Then Joana handed him to Francesc, who held him in his arms and said, *My firstborn, my heir.* And he chose a name for him. Bartomeu. Like his father. He would name the second-born Francesc. Like himself. But they would always call that boy Esteve, because Francesc and Margarida's second baby was sickly and stunted and didn't want to nurse, didn't want to sleep, and didn't want to stop bellowing, his mouth so wide open that all the world's evils entered it, dancing in a line. Joana mumbled, *God and the Virgin Mary, and Reverend Saint Peter, and Reverend Saint John, when traveling the road anon, a gallant wolf they do happen upon. Tell us, gallant wolf, whence are thou headed? To feast on the flesh and the blood of that infant! No, thou shalt not. Get thee to the high mountaintop to kick dust and gnaw on wild scrub!* But while Bartomeu's birth had been a burst of joy, Esteve's birth was a mere whimper of joy. A happiness like an awl that scratched at her on the inside, because Esteve was born with one ear missing. Margarida, night and day, would stubbornly stare at that closed bud on one side of the baby's head, and then she would grab Bartomeu, who was crawling now, undress him, and search and search, unrelentingly, without finding the thing that was missing, convinced that if it was not visible, whatever the family heir lacked must somehow be hidden. And in the end, Joana explained to Francesc that some births were just like that: they made the mother sad.

Joana pulled a wrinkled orange dishcloth embroidered with two cherries off one of the kitchen chairs and tossed it over her shoulder. She let go of the table and made her way over to the counter. She held on to it and she whistled. Three short whistles, one after the other, like a call. She pricked up her ears, and then pulled two dirty knives out of the sink and wiped them on her sleeve. She opened a drawer and grabbed a third knife. From another drawer, filled with candles, she pulled out a skein of poorly wound twine and a hook. She stopped and listened. But she didn't hear the motion she had been expecting, and she gave another high-pitched, commanding whistle. From the final drawer she took a white bag that didn't rip, didn't wear out, and didn't get wet. She shook it open and placed everything in it. When she was ready, she sighed and whistled once more. Through the glazed door to the kitchen came a distracted-looking woman with a smiling, open mouth, seemingly unaware they'd been calling her for some time. Dolça was young, slight, and hairy. She had the friendly face of a goat, an eye that wandered toward her tear duct, buck teeth, a mat of dark hair on her pate, prominent brows that met in the middle of her forehead, and downy hair beneath her nose.

Joana barked: "The washbasins." And Dolça went into the pantry and came out with three—a pink one, a white one, and a green one—and then turned them over to shake out the cobwebs. Joana gestured with her head and Dolça followed her out of the kitchen. They crossed the entryway and exited the house through the main door. The slight morning breeze was nippy. The sun hadn't yet appeared behind the mountains, and the blue slopes were fogged over. In front of the house was a small flagstone threshing floor, splattered with gray and yellow lichen and dried goat shit from when the goats had escaped. In the middle rested a white chair covered in fly droppings, with a striped mauve bolster. When Joana pointed to the chair, Dolça grabbed it by the back and carried it. Marta's gray, horseless carriage was covered in dew. A red path of broken roof tiles led to the house. The two women headed toward one of its side walls, where there was a gray stone laundry lavoir, two empty pots, and a roughly stacked pile of firewood. Farther on there was a tumultuous garden and the outer goat fence, and beyond that was where the trees began. Dolça put the chair down under a chestnut tree and, following a gesture from Joana, filled up the white basin with water from the lavoir. Joana cut a piece of twine and slowly but surely tied the hook to one of the tree's branches. She sat down on the chair, pulled out one small knife and one large one, and sharpened them against each other. When Dolça placed the full basin at her feet, she said, "Bring me a reed." And Dolça went to the garden. She was gone for a long time, but she came back with a piece of reed. Joana put one of the sharpened knives down on the ground. She stuck her hand into the bag and sharpened the third one.

Upstairs, Bernadeta mucked about with her breakfast. She picked up the toast with trembling, worn hands and transparent fingernails. She raised the bread to her mouth, stuck out her pointed tongue, and licked the jam. Just the jam. Then she puckered her lips and scraped the toast with her front teeth, like a rabbit. Margarida turned her head, repulsed, so she wouldn't have to see the nasty things the old woman was doing. The tits chirped so loudly that they could be heard even inside the house. They sang, exhilarated because the darkness had swallowed them up, as it swallows up all things, and then it had spat them out, as it is obliged to spit out all things that awaken stiff and damp. And now they trilled, relieved to reawaken because in the midst of the long night they'd doubted that day would ever come. And they welcomed in the morning, even though it was a glum morn. Margarida didn't like mornings. Because in the morning a naive woman could believe that the night was ending. But night never ended; it merely waited, hiding, and always returned.

Margarida was so dejected after Esteve's birth that she missed the news. They had hanged one of Francesc's brothers, a nineteen-year-old named Joan, in the Plaça de Vic, for being a thief. Before he was executed, he'd told Francesc where he had hidden the stolen shepherds' capes: between two box trees. Francesc had gone looking for them. But as a result of the trial, some inquiries were made, and one fateful morning the solicitor and a group of men came to Mas Clavell for Francesc. The tits chirped. At first Margarida thought they were singing to welcome in the morning. But their chirps were so agitated, so distraught, so insistent, so vexed, that Margarida grew anxious. Francesc was plowing in front of the house when he heard the birds screech and squawk. They shrieked as if possessed, cheep, cheep, cheep, cheep, cheep! They were warning him that the solicitor was coming with his men to seize him and take him away forever for having kept the stolen capes. When Francesc tried to flee, they fired at him six times. Margarida, from the house, felt each shot pierce her own heart, already so small, and, from then on, just a little hunk of chopped meat. God spared him and they hit only his garments, but after that, Francesc took to hiding in the forest.

Margarida would say to him, *Do not flee, do not ever leave.* But he would laugh. As if he were telling a joke only he could understand. *Women cling to places, attaching themselves,* he would respond, *tying themselves up like dogs. To the past, to homes, to children, to things.*

And he would set off happily, turning his back on her. Content to be leaving. He roamed far from the house, first with Bou, and later with more and more men. And Margarida was left alone with all the burdens. With children to raise and fields to sow. With her contemptible mother and her deviant sister who, despite Margarida's endless scolding, was constantly watching the ducks. Evil things! Those drakes that seemed tranquil but whose frenetic orange feet were always moving beneath the water. Fighting with one another, squawking as they all tried to mount the hen at the same time. They would dunk her head; it looked like they were drowning her. Violent, with that shameful coiled genitalia, long, white, and terrible, as they pecked out her neck feathers. If Margarida had taken her husband's side, he would have stayed home. If she had told him he was right. That it was cursed, that house. If she had confessed, pointing at Joana, *It was her. It was my mother. She made a pact with the devil so she could marry my father. She summoned him, Francesc. And she showed him where we live. She pissed on a cross, Francesc! To forswear God and make the Other One come.* Then her husband would have loved her. He would have gently pushed the hair from her face. He would've said, *Margarida, mistress of my house, friend, wife, companion.* But Margarida just watched him leave and stayed silent, her swollen and slothful tongue heavy inside her mouth. And she barely scraped by, abandoned by the light of day, all alone, watching the weeks pass like a woman who'd been buried alive. Until a morning would come, as doleful as all the rest, when she would realize that since she'd endured so many nights of solitude, like a blizzard that had frozen over, the gushing joy of his return must be imminent. Because Francesc always came back. Because they were married and this was his home. And instead of Francesc Llobera, which was the name his father had given him, people would call him Clavell, which was the name she had given him. And then he would arrive. Like the spring, he would arrive. Each time dressed more finely. With stockings up to his knees, and a doublet, and shoes and a hat and a cape, his hair so long it grazed his shoulders. With an entourage of followers who ate his bread and drank his wine and sat around his table. And Margarida would gaze at him, oh, how she would drink him in with her eyes! Filled with a love that flowed from her as he laughed and sang and doled out victuals. She studied him and convinced herself that it must be that when the Lord Our God had chiseled those arms and that torso, when He'd made that mouth and placed teeth inside those lips, God the Father must have also made the traders, haulers, and merchants, the gold and silver coins and the Dutch blue silks for those strapping hands to steal. She told herself that the Lord Our God in all His love made each and every one of the men who traveled with Francesc so he was never lonely, those men who loved him in the way men love one another, which is far better than the way they love women. And that it was He who'd cinched that bunch of leather belts round his waist, armed with short petronels and long petronels, as if He were tying him with a bow. And she would repeat to herself that the Lord had sculpted those intricate and impassable mountains so that Francesc could hide within them. He had opened up paths and conduits so his men could rush down them like torrents. He had carved caves and burrows to contain them and the things they stole. And He had positioned those houses called El Vilar, El Llorà, Masjoan, Mas Riera, Can Muntada, Can Carbassa, and L'Obac so Francesc and his band of men could enter them, force the inhabitants into the kitchen, pull out drawers, rummage through clothes, tear up boards, rip the straw from mattresses, overturn beds and chairs, and find rings, money, chains, spoons, and cups. And she was sure that the Lord Our Father had also provided Francesc's protectors and his safe houses. Banchs, Cortina, Brunyola, the wife of Moner, Puigllaunell, the widow Saavedra, Father Ricard, the parson of Castanyet, and all the others. Who invited Clavell and his band of men to eat at their tables, and offered them places to rest their heads, and brought them eggs, bread, and wine when they were hiding in the forest, and herded sheep behind them to cover their trail so the men pursuing them would not find them.

Bernadeta stuck out a probing tongue and licked the jam remaining on her lips and mustache. She closed her eyes, raised her brows, and flared her nostrils, large as coins. She took a deep sniff. And Margarida could hear the sniffing. And the sound of her big nose inhaling—focused, insistent, and savoring—tore her from the den of her thoughts. Margarida suddenly stood up. She ran to the window, opened it violently, and thrust out her sparrow's head inquisitively. She took in a noseful of air. And she could sense it. Saints preserve us, could she ever. Beneath the scent of a new day, of clean leaves on branches, she discerned the nauseating stench of nether regions. With her eagle eyes, Margarida scrutinized the treacherous green of the trees. She'd known for days that the devil was once again moseying through these woods and circling the house. But she was prepared. Because if the enemy was approaching, if the adversary, if the Cloven-Hoofed, if the Lord of the Flies was drawing near, Margarida would invoke God, Jesus, the Virgin, and all the saints in heaven and all the angels. She would call out to him from the window, *Cowardly murderer, treacherous beast, vulture! Hawk! Thief! Out, out!*, and she would throw at him everything within her reach. She would lob the good cup at his head, and the unbreakable bottle, the lamp, the chair, and the dresser. So God would see how she spurned him. So God would see how she turned her back on him. That she would throw the old woman at him, if need be. It was Bernadeta whom the hawk sought. Before closing the window, the woman, brooding, spat three times.

The sun was up now, but its glow was blanched and plagued by long wisps of fog and a thin, cold rush of wind heading in to intercept it. The goats bleated in their pens. They loosed balls of shit. They shifted their tails. They chased one another. They stood still. They gathered in a cluster. They gnawed on hay and they sniffed. Their udders and nasty bits dangled. The buck's member was small and pointy like a needle. The brown nanny switched her tail and put her ass in his face. The buck smelled it and straddled her from behind, impatient, but he slid off. He lowered his feet. He mounted her again, but again slipped off. Then he clambered up and stayed in place, and they juddered. Atop the golden coach two women lay together. The coach looked better from a distance, because from up close it was clear that the gold was fake, the fabric was cheap, and the whole thing was covered in dust. Blanca—a sturdy old woman with a bovine face, soupy eyes, and a double chin—watched as the brown nanny and the buck fornicated. Elisabet—a skinny middle-aged woman, with the dark eyes of a small carnivore, fallen shoulders, and a long, slender neck—ran her hands over a blue cushion with gilded trim. The white nanny goat and her kid grazed a short stretch farther on, unflappable. Elisabet hadn't been born in that house. She was born in a town by the sea called Castelló d'Empúries. No other woman in that house had ever seen the sea. Except for Margarida. But Margarida said the sea was made of tainted water and blood, and Elisabet didn't know what sea Margarida had seen, because the sea by Roses—and by L'Escala, which was the same sea but on the other side—was blue. Every blue imaginable. Light blue and dark blue, purple blue and bright blue, opaque blue and green blue and blue that seems gray and blue that seems black. And sometimes, depending on how the sun rose or set, and the clouds that accompanied it, the sea could also be gray, or yellow, or orange, or pink, or lilac, or green, or red, with curls of white foam. Elisabet had been married off to the miller of Roses, and from Roses you could glimpse the sea and the snowcapped mountains at the same time. But she hadn't lived in Roses for very long, because the first night she went to sleep at the mill, Elisabet was already pleading with the Virgin to please, oh, please kill her husband. And every morning after, she would pray insistently for that. And when the Virgin killed him, which didn't take Her long, Elisabet threw a party. Within herself. With musicians who played cornemuses. And she grabbed the millhand and they climbed up to the Our Lady of Núria sanctuary to give thanks. But halfway there, Elisabet was struck with fevers, and between Sant Joan de les Abadesses and Ribes de Freser she got the tertian chills. She tried to go on but could not, and she collapsed on the side of the road, drenched and trembling, thinking that rest would help. She lay there until the shivering stopped, and when she sat up, she saw a cherry tree. As if it'd been placed there for her to find when she awoke. Her mouth started to water. She said to the millhand, *Do you want some cherries?* The cherries were hot and sweet and bounteous. Full and red and yellow, so abundant that the birds hadn't been able to peck at them all. If they'd let her and the millhand have their way, they would've eaten until they were sick to their stomachs. But they weren't able to, because a man's voice yelled at them to turn around. The first thing that Elisabet saw was the blunderbuss aimed at them. He had two more hanging from his belt. Then the ravaged boots and the dirty cape, and finally the starved face. That scoundrel robbed the millhand of all he carried, and told him, in a voice that clearly conveyed he'd killed many men, that he would kill him if he ever saw him again. Then he looked at Elisabet and ordered her to follow him. And even though she begged him over and over to let her go, please, to just let her go, let her make her devotions to Núria, for the love of God, that she was a widow. She pleaded with the sweet voice of a good woman, with the damp eyelashes of a poor girl, but the bandolier put a pistol to her chest, cocked the trigger, and said that if she didn't obey, he'd kill her. Elisabet thought it was the end when she fainted from her fever, unable to take another step. Then, rather than shoot her, the man gave her wine from his calabash, and between the drink and the fright Elisabet was no longer quivering. But as she walked behind Clavell, with every step she begged the Virgin to please kill him.

It was Elisabet's fault. That was what he said. The fault of that face, that smell, that mouth as it drank, those hands and those eyes and that hair, that was why he loved her so madly. Hopelessly. She'd stuck a dagger in him. And sickened his heart. He would have married her, he swore. He would have married her even if it meant being an ordinary, poor peasant farmer. He'd married a foolish woman, he explained, everything about her a grievance. He'd married her without loving her, because she was an heiress and had a house, which had turned out to be a barren, sunken, malodorous homestead, cleaved to the earth like a leech. But Elisabet, Elisabet, who had nothing to her name, just that helpless face and that mouth and that gaze, Elisabet he would have married for love. He would tell her, *If you'd met me earlier, when I had a band of over seventy men, you would've loved me then. When I had money and abettors and I swaggered through these mountains—not like a rat, but like a prince—you would've had to love me then.*

Elisabet had tried to escape three times. The first time at Coll del Torn, on Resurrection Sunday. Clavell, seeing that she had fled, forced the local cowherds to search for her, telling them that if they didn't locate her, he'd kill them all. When he found her, he spoke to her like she was a little girl. He told her she couldn't go off on her own. That the mountains were brimming with wild beasts and men who were worse than wild beasts. That once, the men in his gang had found a widow walking with a priest along the king's road. They'd taken her captive and had their way with her. All of them. That in the Mansa woods, near Taradell, they'd found a group of women alone and they'd tied them to the trees and they'd dishonored them many, many times. And that resisting had only made it worse. That a servant girl from the Costa de Vilalleons homestead had put up such a fight that in the end they'd had to give her extreme unction.

The second time she escaped was at Collfred. Clavell forced the local shepherds to look for her. When one of them found her and told the bandolier where she was, Clavell smacked Elisabet's neck so hard that it swelled up like an egg.

The third time was at Conflent. She went off on her own, walking toward Camprodon, because no one would go with her, some fearing Clavell, and others fearing the law. And when he caught up with her, he hit her on the head with a rock, once, twice, and then finally a third time, as if with that rock he wanted to force his way into the only place he couldn't force his way into: her head, filled with insults and seated musicians, cornemuses at the ready—and on that occasion even two violins, and a viola and a double bass—waiting to start the party.

Elisabet soon realized they were walking aimlessly, seeking out shepherds' shelters every three or four days. Sometimes they were charcoal shacks, but Clavell didn't trust the charcoal burners. He knew most of the shepherds. Men with names like Ros or Sastre, Prats or Casasubirana, who, when Clavell asked them to, would kill a sheep and bring the meat to them in the forest. On Fridays they ate only bread. They walked until their victuals ran out and they had to search for another shelter. Sometimes, in the daytime, they knocked on the door of welcoming homesteads. They were invited in, the table was set for them with bread, wine, eggs, soups, bacon, and cabbage, and their calabashes were re-filled. Then they would bring bread, wine, and cured sausage into the forest, and the sons or heir of the homestead would sup with them among the trees. Some would stay for days, and together they would search out a good spot on the king's road. If they saw haulers, merchants, or men on horseback approaching, Clavell would make Elisabet hide in a ditch. When the ill-fated travelers reached the spot where the highwaymen were await-ing them, screams and shots were heard. Sometimes they would allow the travelers to flee, and other times the wounded were still alive when she saw them. Only once did she question what the men had done, and Clavell responded, *Careful you don't get yours too*. They didn't knock when they wanted to be given food at a remote house they were unfamiliar with. They just went in under cover of night. They grabbed provisions of bread and wine while the owners howled in lament, and they slunk back into the woods.

When she started to show, Clavell said it was the fault of the mountains. They were beneath the peak of Les Agudes. That the Montseny makes pregnant women lose their good sense. He walked in front and she behind, thinking she would die from hunger. And thinking she would welcome that. Because then she wouldn't have to see the face of that child planted by a sinful seed. And she and the baby, dead inside her, as if already buried, would decompose nicely into fertilizer. And from it would grow trees. Oaks, beeches, and almond trees, anything but a cherry tree. Sometimes Clavell would exclaim that the baby would be named Francesc, like him, because his second son, whom he had already named Francesc, was a child so unworthy of the name that everyone called him Esteve. Other times he would cry and shout, *Burn, burn, burn, I'll burn down the entire Montseny!* And she thought if only he would burn it down, for that way they'd be found. Which is why he had her brought to the Sanctuary of Sant Segimon. Because he said that Elisabet was enamored of the mountains, that she didn't eat and didn't speak and had eyes only for the forest. Clavell knew the hermits and lay brothers there, who all had the same blue fingernails and the same sugar-coated voices, with which, one morning, they told Elisabet she had to leave. *You have to leave*, they said. *They've captured Clavell and they've executed him and you cannot stay here any longer.* And the musicians could throw only a paltry, deplorable party, because Elisabet didn't know where to turn, or where to go, alone in the middle of the forest, with that belly that was a deadweight, and with her feet swelling up, cracking open, and bleeding rotten black blood.

She slept curled up like a common shrew. Sheltered by the trees, imagining which creature would devour her like a stuffed partridge. When she opened her eyes, the fog had come in but she wasn't dead. She was freezing because her drenched skirts and cape scarcely covered her belly. The forest was white and gray, and the air seemed made of silver. Then she caught a whiff of burning firewood, which smelled good, as if you could eat the very scent off the wind. She imagined charcoal burners working and she sat up. The morning was so thick that she couldn't see her hands. She walked clutching the trees that appeared suddenly, like elbows and arms to hold on to. And she didn't realize that the smoke wasn't from a charcoal burner but from a chimney until was standing right in front of the house.

The buck and the nanny goat separated. Each went their own way. And Blanca, atop the coach, got onto all fours. She smiled, then approached Elisabet's ankles. She stuck her head beneath her skirt to smell her, and she stroked her with her forehead and with her nose and with her cheeks. Elisabet, who was resting on one elbow, lay down on her back. Then Blanca tucked up Elisabet's clothes, pulling on them with her mouth, until Elisabet could open her legs like a gully. And suddenly Blanca's hands appeared, two ferrets, welcome trailblazers, and Elisabet had to abandon her thoughts, because those ferrets shimmied up her crests and stroked them, they descended into her valleys and devoured all they found there. Mice and moles and snakes, squirrels and rabbits and sparrows. They gobbled them up whole. Skin, feathers, bones, and entrails. Elisabet moaned, but they were still hungry. They scrambled up and down trees, searching for eggs, and when Elisabet trapped those wild and fleshy little beasts, when she caught them, she would grip them by the scruff of the neck— Blanca's wrists—and bring them up to the nests so they could eat all the little chicks.

The door that led out of the pens was metal and had wheels. It opened with a rasp, and Àngela appeared. She was a poorly fashioned woman, hunchbacked; she looked younger than Blanca, older than Elisabet, with yellow hair, her jaw out of joint, her nose bent, and her legs twisted. She was limping. She looked at the two women resting on the coach, one on top of the other, and without flinching said, "They want the kid." Àngela spoke like someone who has a blockage or a pit inside her mouth. Then she went through the gate and approached the goats to grab the animal, who was bleating.

When Joana saw them coming from behind the house, Àngela carrying the kid, followed by Elisabet and Blanca, she rolled up her sleeves. And then everything happened very quickly. They put the animal down upon the earth as an offering. It went beee, beee. The women formed a circle. Joana, her ass up at the edge of the white chair, flipped the animal onto its side, and with a length of cord she tied up its legs. Àngela, Elisabet, and Blanca knelt and placed their hands on the kid. They held it down. It was calm. As if it didn't know that animals could die, on a cool, fresh morning, surrounded by women's hands. Dolça placed the pink basin beneath its chin. Joana reached for one of the sharpened knives laid out on the ground and made a precise slit in its neck. And the kid emitted a sound that to Àngela seemed one of pain, to Elisabet one of fear, to Dolça one of pleasure, and to Blanca one of surprise. Joana had no opinion on the matter. To her it was just a sound of being killed, with eyes open and tongue out. The basin filled with blood. So scarlet it was almost black. The kid shivered. Blanca and Elisabet held its legs. Àngela pulled up its hot, fuzzy face.

"It's dead," she said, pensive and serious, because you die only once. And Àngela, who was an unfeeling woman, would've liked to feel the pain and scream a lot when she died. To moan with her tongue out and grind her teeth, and tremble, and have a big, suppurating, tattered wound that bled all over, and to stick her fingers into it, and dig and dig, and shriek and cry, and understand all that she hadn't understood, all that she should've understood. And to take the hand of Martí the Tenderhearted and tell him, *I finally understand, Martí.*

Dolça set the blood to one side. Joana tossed the knife into the white basin and picked up another. She brought the animal closer and made an incision on one of its back legs. She inserted a reed into the hole she had just opened up, and blew. The animal's skin inflated. Then she turned it over. She made a vertical cut on its jaw, and others on each leg. *Explain it to me*, Àngela would ask, once they were hidden. Martí the Tenderhearted would murmur, *It's like when you get pricked, or cut, or burned*. Joana was peeling the animal's leg as if she were undressing it. When it was clean, she gestured for Àngela to hang the kid from the hook on the tree. Still in the chair, Joana washed the knives in the basin of water, dunked her hands, rinsed them, and dried them with the dishcloth with the cherries on it that was draped over her shoulder. She stood up slowly, hands resting on her knees. She went over to the hanging animal and, with expert fingers, separated the skin from the filmy white fat on the flesh, which was pink, shiny, and muscular, yellow on the belly, purple on the legs. When she reached its head, she undressed the skull. Its chestnut eyes were left bulging amid the fat and bone. Joana threw the skin a short distance away, hairy and dry on one side, damp and greasy on the other. Martí would say, *Like tickles, like caresses—* Martí and Àngela would be lying in their hideout—*but on the flip side*. They were the same age because they'd been born at almost the same time. But Àngela didn't understand him; when her first teeth came in, she ate a quarter of her own tongue and chewed her fingers down until you could see the bone, and Margarida had had to make her some gloves. Joana ran the dishcloth with the cherries over the animal's flesh, as if she were drying it. She made a cut beneath its tail, in the direction of its belly. She slit open its tummy, filled with gray and blue organs, which spilled out. She released them from the films that bound them. They were a sticky tangle, steaming and clean, that she placed in the green basin. With her hands inside the kid, gripping tightly, she pulled on its kidneys, covered in fat that she then peeled off. She opened up its chest and pulled out its lungs and heart. *Are you hurting me?* Àngela would ask. With the big knife, Joana sliced off the animal's head. Martí the Tenderhearted replied, *Yes*. Then Joana hacked the animal's body in two. And then into quarters. But Àngela couldn't feel it. Martí would ask, *What about here?* But no. She could feel only the weight, the roughness of his little animal hands, the friction, the cadence, the agitated blood, Martí's hands on her body, Martí's mouth, so close to her ear, saying, *And now?* Saying, *And here?* Saying, *Like this?*

MIDDAY

Ahora que estoy muerta, me he dado tiempo para pensar.*

JUAN RULFO, *PEDRO PÁRAMO*

The sun climbed to the middle of the sky, white and frosty, as if naked. The red path lay like a snake in front of the house, the trees' tallest leaves received the wind's dispirited caress, and the house closed its eyes and stuck out its face so the delicate rays would lick its facade.

Blanca and Elisabet brought the pieces of the kid into the kitchen. Joana, the bag and the knives. Dolça, the blood. Àngela threw the dirty water from the basin over some scrub brush, and carried the skin and viscera back inside. They would make browned goat gravy stew, goat lungs, goat forcemeat, goat offal, and goat-blood fritters. Joana orchestrated the bedlam. She ordered them to peel and cut garlic and onions. To grab a pinch of salt pork from the pantry. To bring flour and eggs and add them to the blood to make the fritters. To pull pots and a jar from

---

* Now that I'm dead, I've had time to think.

the cabinets, and to fill the jar with oil and the pots with water. Joana ceremoniously lit the four black flowers. Like some kind of magic. They bloomed with petals that were blue flames. Into a pot they dunked one of the kid's thighs, its head, split in two with the tongue hanging out, and a bit of stolen salt pork. In another they soaked the heart, the spleen, the kidneys, the liver, and the lungs. They put them on the fire. In the third, they scalded the offal. When the oil in the pot was boiling, they poured in spoonfuls of blood mixed with eggs and flour, which crackled. And Joana said, "Once upon a time there was a poor young man and a rich heiress who fell in love. The young couple very much wanted the marriage to go forward, but her parents could not accept their daughter marrying a have-not, and they told her, *We won't allow it!*"

Joana's voice was deep and scratchy.

"But they continued courting, and one evening, as the young man was returning home, sad after spending time with her, he ran into an old woman who asked him, *What befell you, my boy, that's made you so sulky?* He replied that he'd been courting, but that he and his beloved could not marry. *Why not?* asked the old woman. *Because her parents don't want us to, I am not of their standing.*"

The women listened as they cut up the rest of the kid. The legs, split. The ribs, separated. The neck, chopped.

"*Do you two love each other?* asked the old woman. And the young man answered, *More than you can imagine. But what good does that do us? Who knows! I have some herbs that might help you. Isn't it true that when you go over to court her, her parents offer you a drink? Well, here, take this herb. Spread it at the top of the stairs, and when her parents go down to the cellar for wine, make sure they step on it. And here, have a small bunch of this other herb, which will cure them when you decide the time is right.*"

When the fritters were done, the women used a bit of the oil to fry up garlic and brown the pieces of kid. They set them aside, and in the same oil they sautéed some onion. In the meantime, they mixed chopped-up dried bread with vinegar, thyme, and rosemary in another pot. They poured in some of the broth from the boiled entrails, two beaten eggs, honey, and cinnamon, and added it to the fire. Then they dipped the goat into the mixture.

"Saturday afternoon came around, and the young man, dressed better than ever, went to woo his beloved. When her mother set eyes on him, she shouted, *Boy, surely a drink would hit the spot?* The young man accepted, and while the woman searched for the spouted jug, the two lovers scattered the herbs at the top of the staircase. And when the old woman went down into the cellar, she stepped right on them. But oh, oh, daughters of mine! As soon as her feet crushed them, she began to fart long and loudly!"

The women in the kitchen went wild. Dolça laughed like a goat. Elisabet, like a ferret. Àngela, like a boar. Joana, like a mare. And Blanca opened her mouth like a calf and stomped and clapped to make a ruckus.

"The mother was walking down the steps and she had to stop and rest to give the farts time to get out. What a wild rumpus! One after the other. Like a series of thunderclaps on a blustery day, a pot full of boiling cabbages!" The women shrieked. "Whatever will you do now! the mother said to herself. What a predicament! How will you get out of this one? Oh, it shan't be easy! Terrified as she was, she called for her husband. He came to her aid, but as he walked down the stairs, he, too, stepped on the herbs, and then, my daughters, he, too, started farting up a storm. He took the stairs two by two, but the farts came three by three. And when he reached the cellar, he found his wife, who, like him, was so gassy she couldn't even speak. They hugged each other, and it was impossible to know which one was more flatulent! *However will we get out of here?* she exclaimed. *They'll have to drag me!* he said. *What's going on down there, why haven't you come back up?* asked their daughter from the kitchen. *Oh, my Lord, God help us!* they screamed from the cellar. The young lovers went down the stairs, careful not to step on the herbs, and they found her father and mother, red as embers, farting."

The women were crying. The kitchen had filled with the spiced and sweet, oily, delicious smell of the onion, the cinnamon, the vinegar, the grease, and the fat.

"*Whatsover is the matter?* the young woman asked. *Oh, Lord, we can't hold in our farts!* her parents shouted. *Never you fear!* exclaimed the young man. *For I have an herb that can stop them. Give it to us!* they pleaded, but the young man replied that he would not give it to them unless they allowed him to marry their daughter. When the old couple agreed, the young man spread out the second herb on the ground so they could stamp on it, and the lovers were married."

The women burst into laughter, shouts, shrieks, and applause so raucous and shrill that they reached upstairs, where Margarida was sitting, angry because there was no way to get any rest in that house. What with those women and these women. What with the racket in the kitchen and Marta's labored bustling about; she never had enough, all morning, turning on and off tools that whistled, beeped, flipped over, and banged. And insistently asking, Bernadeta, do you want to go out, do you want to go downstairs, do you want to go see the goats. A little while earlier, shameless Marta had been sitting on the floor like an infidel with her eyes closed and her hands on her folded knees, breathing as if she'd never learned how. The little mirror rested at her feet, and the musicians that lived inside were playing infernal songs.

Oh, how the women laughed, boisterous and churlish, the first time they saw Marta on that carpet, on all fours and moving like a cat. Ass out, ass in. Ass up, ass down. Spreading her legs in ways a woman shouldn't. Soon she was making heretical sounds, *Ohhhm, ohhhm, ohhhm*, inhaling and exhaling so slowly it was exasperating. Margarida sighed, depleted, because the only thing she wanted was to rescue that final day from the ruins of her memory. The farewell. The last time she saw her husband. But all these women broke her concentration. They beleaguered her. And she was incapable of distinguishing, of separating, Francesc's last visit from his other errant, random, capricious visits, miserly as onion peels.

The more he left, the longer it would take him to return. And the more men in his band, and the more rings, and the more capes, and the more pursuers behind him—the bailiffs of Osor and Rupit with their squads, the duke of Feria and his soldiers— the more handsome Francesc became. And the more handsome he became, the less he loved Margarida. And the more shameless, nasty, stupid, and simple the women of the house seemed to him. And the more tedious and fusty the house itself seemed to him. And the dirtier the children. And the stinkier the entryway, which gave him a headache the instant he set foot inside. He would look at Margarida with eyes overflowing with disdain. And he would compare her. She knew he was comparing her. To those other weaselly floozies. Even now Margarida would sometimes worry that those other stolen women were by Francesc's side in heaven. Anastàsia Colobrans or Maria Serradora, thieving ferrets. But then she'd convince herself they weren't there with him. Surely not. Heavens no! God doesn't forgive women who lie with men who don't belong to them. He doesn't want them. Like He hadn't forgiven Elisabet. Bitter venom. Dungheap of vices. Although when Elisabet died, making faces and pissing blood, Margarida's heart had clenched so she couldn't even breathe. Because Elisabet had died first. Slippery snake. She was always a step ahead of her, even in that. And how terrifying for poor Margarida, just imagining Elisabet and Francesc meeting up again. In heaven. And that God would marry them up there. But she needn't have worried. No. Because God wants nothing to do with such slatternly women. With women who sully. Women like beasts. Contrary to nature. Those who lie with other women's men and keep what isn't theirs. Because Elisabet had seduced Francesc like a spider. She had gotten inside him, like venom, into his eyes, his mouth, his ears, and his heart, and like that—poisoned, blind, and deaf as she had him—she'd throttled his memory so he would forget his children and his wife, and she'd kept him all for herself, until she'd made him lose everything. Even his luck.

In the end, he would come alone. When he came at all. He would leave his men in the woods near the house. He'd sit down at the table and look at the children until they started to cry. He would grab Bartomeu and repeat many times that no matter what anyone said, he was his father. *Don't forget, don't forget your father.* Francesc didn't even look at Esteve, but the child whimpered just the same. When night fell, he would drag himself to the bed like a condemned man. He would stretch out on top of Margarida with his eyes closed and poke her with his serpent-headed shameful bit. The only thing that Our Lord had made ugly in Francesc. And no matter what her mother said, it was nothing like eating mushrooms. When he was finished, he would curl up and say, *God has forsaken me.* But God hadn't forsaken him. God, who had let them flay the lamb, who had let them make a martyr of His son: God had chosen him. God had taken him up to Glory with Him. He had reached out for Francesc's sturdy hands, and

He had kissed them. He had kissed his pearly mouth. His hands, forgiven. His lips, forgiven. And ten more kisses. One for each finger. Forgiven. God covered Francesc's supple and toasted skin with kisses. Arms and forehead and neck, forgiven. Because God had him by His side. Margarida knew that. Because you can see the path only as a martyr. Like the lamb. Only from repentance. Only from split-open loins and two bloody holes where your ears should be.

What God had abandoned was the house. And the women who lived inside it, crammed in like roaches, He'd forsaken them. Like He had forsaken the infants born during the Passion. Because while Christ's torment lasted, the shredded feet of the Messiah climbing Calvary Hill, his torn back carrying the cross, his long hair, dripping sweat and blood, God just looked at His son, He loved only and cried only for the lamb. He wasn't there for anyone else. And all the men and women born during the Passion were left with the bad part. Haunted. Neglected. Forever. Disregarded, discounted, condemned. And things that are punished never die.

And God had so abandoned those women that, one dark day, Margarida came upon the root of all evil, he who climbs mountains more easily than you can walk across a plain, there in the vegetable patch. Stealing turnips. The peaks had awoken covered with early snow, and the trees crackled. That morning the sky had clouded over and hail fell mixed with snow, and then just snow, and then the sun was beaming and it was snowing at the same time. It had already occurred to Margarida that such weather was the devil's doing, but she was nevertheless caught unawares. The snow smelled clean, and the poor woman did not catch a whiff of the adversary's stench. She thought he was from Francesc's gang. He was dressed as a man. Ugly and weedy, just nose, ears, and a big mouth. He was piercing the snow with his villainous red hands. Margarida shouted at him, *Hey, you!*— scaring him—*Where's Clavell?* The lurcher's expression conveyed at first surprise, then satisfaction. In a clear, simple voice, he said, *Clavell will not return, because they are hunting him with ever-increasing persistence and most of his men are already dead.* He pulled up a turnip round as a fist and added, *And because he has another woman now.* Margarida's chest writhed like a nest of snakes, and she caught a whiff of nether regions, of feet, of rot, of decadence, and of goat. May God forgive her. May God forgive her, because instead of making the sign of the cross, instead of throwing rocks at him or handfuls of frozen snow, instead of chasing him off like a dog, shouting, *Cowardly murderer, treacherous beast, vulture! Hawk! Enemy! Thief! Out, out!* and opening her heart to the Lord, to the Virgin and the angels, begging for salvation, she listened. *I will tell you something you want to know in exchange for every turnip.* The name of the woman traveling with him was Elisabet. The malevolent yanked up another tuber. She was a woman of good height, pleasing appearance, white face, and dark life. She had been heading to Núria to marry a millhand in secret, but between Sant Joan de les Abadesses and Ribes de Freser, she swapped him out for Clavell. Margarida kept ruminating, the thirsty have water here, water from the heart of Jesus, who is a well of fresh water, the more water you scoop from it, the more water there is, and the purer and clearer. But when Clavell wanted to give her back to her family, Elisabet refused to leave him, and the wagging tongues claimed she'd sworn to kill herself if Francesc left her side. The black beast cradled his arms to make a basket for all those turnips.

Just as the devil had predicted, Francesc did not return. And when the viceroy's men ripped off the doors of the house, asking,

Where is Clavell? Where have you hidden him?, Margarida replied, *I don't know*, which was the truth. They dragged out the children, the mother-in-law, the simple sister-in-law, and the bandolier's wife, and brought them to the threshing floor, and they made them watch as they burned the hayrick and the granary, as they salted the garden and the fields, as they chopped down the holm oaks and girdled the oak and chestnut trees, as they slit the throats of the herd and entered the house on horseback with torches so that Clavell could never again take refuge there.

Margarida told them, *Clavell has another woman*. But Francesc's last visit was already showing on her belly. They responded, *You are the mother of his children*. They took her. And Margarida prayed, please, for them to kill her quickly. Instead, they tied her behind one of the horses and dragged her down a never-ending path sown with claws. And then she heard it. Unmistakable as a thunderbolt deep in her ears. The voice of Our Lord, who told her, *Get away from me, wicked woman*. The terrible clamor came from between the haunches of the mount: *Enter the fires of hell, primed for you by the devil and his ministers. Off into the shadows with the snake that never rests.* And as they climbed through mountains of manure and fire, and descended through valleys of embers where the wind bellowed and the trees covered in magpies and crows screeched, the incessant voice whipped her, *I sculpted you and yet you have taken another master*, so deafeningly that the woman could scarcely distinguish the words. *Away, fiend, for I gave you ears and you listened to another*. Margarida looked in terror at the horse's ass and shook her head. *I gave you a mouth and you conspired with another*. She was tongue-tied but the clamor continued, *I gave you eyes and you looked toward darkness*.

Then poor, wretched Margarida realized that it was not the viceroy's men who were carrying her off. These were demons. She observed the sides of that terrible road and saw rows of flayed beasts left out in the sun. Channels of blood and fetid entrails that nourished vegetables planted in rotting earth. She could glimpse the sea of blood and tainted waters. And hell's walls of fire and stone, flanked by throngs of deformed demons supplied with all sorts of weapons. Bellows, cauldrons, pans, knives, grills, axes, burins, weeding hoes. She heard them laughing, and from atop the walls and the watchtowers they shouted, *Tie her up! Bind her, not her hands, bind her heart!*, while the doors, which were fiery mouths, swallowed her. Hell had a hundred thousand towers and streets and furnaces and wells of burning eyes, where banished souls were decapitated and quartered, punctured and roasted, battered and whipped, digested yet still vomited up, ravished and hung by their tongues and genitals, melted like lard in huge pans, to later be pummeled with mallets and clubs, manipulated with red-hot tongs, and fashioned into horrible shapes. Those demons dumped Margarida into a sinister jagged gullet, and they dragged her through corridors arrayed with niches and spiky stairs that stank of rotten flesh and dung. Screams could be heard everywhere. The dragging of chains. Voices that emitted all sorts of blasphemies and impure words. Some cursed their tongues, their eyes, their hands; others cursed their parents, their circumstances, the moment when they'd been condemned. They grunted and growled, bemoaning their torment, and saying, *Where did you get that from, accursed hands?! I made a mistake, I got lost!*

The viceroy's soldiers locked Margarida in the Veguer prison. In a cell with half a dozen other condemned souls and hordes of rats. The sun came up, and they didn't see it. It set, and they didn't see it. Because the female prisoners were never allowed out. The yard and the window with bars on it were only for the men. Margarida's belly kept growing in the dark, like a rotting thing, a thing swelling up and filling with juices and flies. She got down on her knees and asked Our Lord to forgive her. To come rescue them. Her and the child she carried within. To curtail their suffering. Not to put more on her plate than she could possibly eat. But, as if she were a liar, as if she were deceitful and her prayers and pleading all false, she gave birth like an animal. At night and in silence. Covered in sweat, streaming blood and filth that weren't even visible. And when the other prisoners heard it, all of them whores, procuresses, and poisoners, all of them misshapen and monstrous from all the stench and all the darkness and all the evil deeds, all of them murderers of their own children and of their own parents and of their husbands, they rushed to help her. *Sssh*, they said, and they felt her belly and they held her hands and they brushed the hair out of her face. Opened, with her ass in the air and the baby halfway out, squatting, pissing, and shitting herself, Margarida shouted blindly. Asking, please, for them to catch Francesc and kill him cruelly and slowly, so he would have time to think of her. And for them to also capture and kill, just as cruelly and slowly, the weasel traveling with him. The baby slid out, covered in the dark liquids that come out of women. When the jailer heard its cries, he opened the cell door. A streak of light entered the cell, and one of the women with hot hands who was caring for Margarida as she expelled the placenta said, *This little one's got the face of a fox.* The jailer locked the door again and Margarida remained very still, waiting for the baby boy to die, without giving him a name, so she wouldn't grieve too much when the rats gnawed off his fingers.

When they asked Elisabet how it had happened, how they'd caught Clavell, she shrugged. Margarida imagined them arm in arm. Elisabet glowing. It wasn't just her belly; you could see it in her eyes, in her allure: she was pregnant. They'd knocked at the door of a welcoming house. Widow Saavedra or Mother Bou. The woman's children had gone down and opened the door, Francesc had come in, Elisabet had stayed outside, and a little while later one of the daughters had brought some food out to her. Then, amid tears, they'd bid each other farewell, and Francesc had embraced her and said, *Elisabet, mistress of my house, friend, wife, companion.* A servant had taken Elisabet to Sant Segimon, and Francesc had stayed in that house, where, to save their own necks, some of his men would sell him out. They would shoot him in the back, tie him up, and deliver him to the militia. And a doctor from Santa Coloma de Farners would stitch him up and keep him alive so they could hand him over to the viceroy's men.

They took him to the Veguer prison and the rabble made up a song for him. *Little girls cry, cry with sadness, because Clavell is now imprisoned*, they trilled. But they didn't let Francesc and Margarida see each other. As if they were no longer husband and wife, as if God's laws meant nothing. As if Margarida were behind bars on her own merits. And when they wrote down all the things that Francesc had confessed, after invoking Our Lady of Montserrat so they would stop the tortures, all his crimes and the others they found convenient to pin on him, they condemned him as a bandolier, as the leader of a gang, as a thief, as a highwayman and a murderer. And they sentenced him to a hundred lashes, and ordered his ears to be cut off, for him to be flaunted in a cart, tortured with hot tongs, and then drawn and quartered.

They took him out on a donkey and they whipped him in the Plaça del Blat, on the Carrer de la Bòria, in the Plaça de la Llana, on the Carrer dels Calderers, in the Placeta d'en Marcús, on the street and square called Montcada, behind the Palau de la Reina, on the Carrer dels Encants, on the Carrer Ample, on the Carrer del Regomir, on the Carrer de la Ciutat, in the Plaça de Sant Jaume.

One hundred times. His back split open like a slaughtered pig on butchering day. They sought out his ears amid his knotted hair—they found them there, like two snails, and they cut them off. The blood ran down his neck, down his shoulders, burbling. They brought out red-hot pincers and they ripped off the flesh of his loins, like birds pecking at his cadaver. But he wasn't dead, not yet. And he screamed. He screamed and screamed, unashamed to scream, while the people who watched his execution from the street, and from all the windows and all the balconies, licked their lips, because the fat coming into contact with the red-hot iron smelled like bacon. Then he lost consciousness. All covered in red, scarlet, and black blood, and the only thing he didn't notice was the four horses splitting his chest into four parts. Then they paraded him around. In pieces. Along the city streets. They displayed his hands, each one on its own, on different streets, never, ever having been so alone. And the ill, the wounded, the lame, the broken children, they ran Clavell's fingers with their purple nails over their ulcers, lumps, stumps, and heads, so he would carry off the pain, the illness, the hurt, carry it all along with him to hell. When they displayed his feet, each one on its own, on different streets, never, ever having been so alone, toothless children kicked them and spat on them. When they displayed his head, people plucked out hairs to make relics. And when he was bald, they stuck his head into a cage and they hung it from one of the towers on the Sant Antoni Gate, with his eyes open, so he could see what he no longer had to see. *Anima eius requiescat in pace. Amen.*

Then Marta told Bernadeta that she'd brought her lunch up to her, but if she wanted to eat she'd have to get out of bed and sit at the table in the parlor. The house filled with a damp, warm smell of reheated vegetables and steeped chicken bones. Margarida, who was still twiddling her thumbs, stopped and grasped her elbows with her hands. Marta helped Bernadeta out of bed. She had brought her a glass of water, a plate of soup, a napkin, and a spoon. The parlor was a large square space and had a window with a stone bench and a small false balcony, just a foot long. The walls were white, the beams dark and riddled with wormholes, and the floor was of warm brown tiles. There was a solid table surrounded by chairs where no one ever ate. Just Bernadeta, on the days when she didn't feel like going downstairs. The old woman sat down and coughed. A small cough. She sighed. She situated her nose over her plate, picked up the spoon very slowly, with spotted, veiny hands made of glass, and submerged it in the soup. She brought it to her partly open mouth. She stretched her lips and slurped. Focused. She inhaled and dipped the spoon in again. She pulled it out, methodically. She spilled half the broth along the way, and swallowed. Marta asked if the soup was good, and Bernadeta made a throaty sound that meant yes. Then Marta added that Alexandra would be stopping by at some point after lunch to pick up clothes. And Rosa would come by like she did every afternoon, but with her kids, because David, her husband, had had an accident with the truck. Bernadeta slurped, drinking the bit of liquid she'd successfully conveyed, and exhaled. The kids will stay in the kitchen and do their homework, said Marta. And she explained that Rosa's husband had emerged without a scratch, but the truck, filled with pigs on their way to the slaughterhouse, had tipped over and many pigs had died. Some from the scare and some because they were piled up and couldn't breathe, and a few escaped and ran into the mountains and they were still looking for them. David had to go speak with the insurance company, and that's why the kids were coming with Rosa. Bernadeta wasn't listening.

The women in the kitchen pulled out the thigh, the half head, and the bit of salt pork from the bubbling pot, and they separated the meat from the bones. The tongue from the mouth. The brain from the skull. They chopped it all up very fine and they put it back on the fire, with its juice and dry bread, milk, pepper, and eggs. There were two flies on the window. Chasing each other. Now they landed on the wall, now on the table, now on the countertop. They were two black spots, with golden butts and gray wings, buzzing. They licked their hairy legs and then rubbed them together. The first fly had spread its wings wide but wasn't flying. The second approached. First tentatively, then closer and closer. Until one climbed onto the back of the other and they remained like that, stacked. Both with immense eyes and still wings. Delicate and discreet. As if they weren't touching. But they were touching. As if they weren't rubbing up against each other. But they were rubbing up against each other. Blanca was watching it.

Margarida said to her, *Nasty girl, worse than nasty!* and *Deviant!* and *Don't look, don't look!* because Blanca was looking. She would watch the pigs, who were hot, hairy, and heavy, with rough, wet snouts and small, shiny eyes. They snuffled and ate. They scraped at the ground of the pen surreptitiously and then scratched themselves. The boar's head under the sow's belly. The boar's nape under the sow's jowls. And then they would line up, and the boar would lick her ass under her tail. The sow had a thick neck, hard buttocks, and a wet, protuberant slit that festered. The boar had a hunched back, immense loins, and a dangly pink bit that was skinny and curled like a worm. He awkwardly managed to mount her, but his aim was poor. The sow's gash awaited him. They grunted. The sow was still, with all four hooves on the ground. The boar rose up, leaning over her as if he were very tired, as if they'd been making love for centuries. And then he found the spot, and there were short, rapid thrusts, until Margarida shouted, *Nasty, nasty girl, deviant!* But despite Margarida's scolding, Blanca would watch.

The female cat stretched and whimpered, her ass in the air and her tail to one side. The male observed her from a certain distance and suddenly drew near, bit into her nape, and gripped it. He held her against the ground and she yelped. Quelled, she moved her legs. Then they were still, tense, withdrawn, and focused, one atop the other. Huddled close. He nibbled on her ears. Until suddenly they separated. They chased, hissed, and scratched each other.

No one scolded Blanca once the viceroy's men had burned down the house and carried off Margarida, because all Joana did was laugh and all Bartomeu and Esteve did was cry. And the only thing that was heard inside that black, crumbling house was laughter, sobs, and the grumbling of starving tummies. Blanca made no sound, so as not to scare off the creatures she was watching. The roe deer had thin legs, small heads, black eyes, white butts. First they chased each other and then they remained still. The male would get up close to the female and sniff her butt and her folds. He would lick her a little, with a pastel-pink tongue, and they would walk more. Then he'd lick her more, and they would walk even more. Until the male would climb up onto her as if he weighed nothing, but the female would shake him off. They would walk. And try again. Up. And down. And he would lick her. And he would climb up again, and she would move ahead, and he would fall, and he would lick her, and he would climb up, and down, and then they were done. The foxes went tick-tick-tick with their quick feet. They sought each other out, bodies crouching and tails dragging. They would play. They would draw close and then part, close and then part. The female rubbed her white neck on the ground, frisky, she shook and stuck her ass near the male's nostrils, he shrieked and mounted her. Excited. They moved their hips frenetically, ears lowered, eyes round and yellow, and mouths open. And when they finished they wanted to detach, but they didn't. They couldn't! They were trapped inside each other. And they made clumsy somersaults, then were tranquil, then giddy, sniffing and scratching the earth, stuck together by their naughty bits, each trying to go their own way. The hares chased each other. And suddenly they turned. They stood up, they faced each other, they swatted each other with their front paws, pfuu-pfuu-pfuu, it seemed like they didn't want each other, but they did want each other, because suddenly one of them would glue their head beneath the other's neck, their face to the soft underbelly of the other, and one would lay their belly flat against the ground, lift their butt up high, and the other would climb onto their back, four ears in the air, and they would shiver deliriously.

One of Clavell's men went up to the house to tell the women. But when he saw the house destroyed, the fields and the trees ravaged, he shouted, *Bastards! Vipers! Scum!* He went into the moldering entryway, still howling, *Bastards! Vipers! Scum!* And he didn't stop shouting until he found Blanca, Joana, and the children in the kitchen, curled up and bristling like cats. He said his name was Miquel Paracolls, that he was from Malla, and he'd come up to tell them that it was over. That they'd executed Clavell. Joana laughed like a donkey. She was sitting on her bench, which was the only thing the viceroy's men hadn't flattened, and Paracolls looked at her with alarm. The old woman lay in a puddle of her own piss, her skirt black with flies, and the esparto grass cushion beneath it rotted. Her cheek, an eye, and her mouth drooped, because the terrifying sight of the house burning and the sound of Margarida's screams as they carried her off had given Joana apoplexy. She couldn't move her right arm, or her right leg, and she could scarcely speak; she only laughed every once in a while, as if the viceroy's men had also entered her head, with torches and on horseback. Blanca gave some nettle soup to Miquel Paracolls from Malla, and the man ate it eagerly, without a spoon, and sitting on the floor, because not a single chair was left intact. He had a small head, hair like straw, red gums, and white teeth. And Blanca thought he looked like a dog. When he finished eating, the man cried. He furrowed his brow, contorted his mouth, and opened up a small hole between his lips, whence emerged a torn voice that said that the viceroy's troops had torn off the doors of all the abettors, of all the nearby farmhouses, welcoming or not. That in Roda de Ter they'd killed half the men accused of hiding Clavell. No one else had wanted to come up to the house to see if the women and children were alive, or whether the house was still standing, because they were all dead, or dead scared, same difference. But there were two separate things. The voice and the man. The dog and the things he said. *I was affronted*, he yelped, *my father died, and one of our neighbors, named Antoni Maneja, caused me offense. Because my father had owed wheat to this Maneja, and when the old man died, the bastard took all the wheat he wanted.* He was sobbing. He crawled on all fours over to Blanca, and explained that later he'd gone to find Clavell and he'd asked him to kill Maneja. They'd shot Maneja twice. One shot after the other. At the door to his house. Then they'd burned the farmhouse and stables. Paracolls's tongue was wet and his snout was filled with snot. He was dripping drool and tears. Blanca took his head in her hands, and she stuck a finger into the small hole where the words came out. His lips were chapped. The flesh inside was hot and wet. The weepy and pathetic trickle of his voice stopped. She stroked his gums, which were thin and slippery. His dog teeth were pointy. The children and Joana pretended to sleep. Blanca introduced another finger. His tongue moved of its own accord. Miquel Paracolls, like a puppy, licked her fingers. Wagged his tail. He closed his eyes and sucked. His warm tongue searched between her thumb and index finger, between her ring and middle fingers, and then Blanca tucked up her skirt. She stuck him underneath, so he could smell her, like a bitch. She rammed her buttocks into his face, so he would kiss her ass, first softly, with a delicate tongue, then quickly, with an impetuous tongue. Because Blanca wanted that man to come up very close behind her, with his pink bits, small but hard, the way dogs come up very close behind bitches, with their pink bits, sticking out thirsty tongues. Miquel Paracolls from Malla howled. Their thighs banged together, impatient, the thumps were relentless, the bitch wanted more, and the thumping was so hard, so brutal, that their legs trembled.

The door to the kitchen opened and Marta went in. She pushed it with her butt because she was carrying Bernadeta's empty lunch tray. The women fished out the heart, spleen, liver, kidneys, and lungs from another pot, and cut them into strips. Marta put the tray down on the counter. She went into the pantry. She came back out with a plate covered in a translucent membrane and placed it inside the glass urn. The women fried the heart, spleen, liver, kidneys, and lungs, and added raw onion and a little bit of the cooking broth, dry bread, and more vinegar and herbs, a great deal of herbs. They also cut the intestines into strips, and they boiled them again. When the bell rang, Marta ripped the membrane off the plate and held it with the tips of her fingers because it was so hot. She brought it to the table, filled a glass with water, and sat down. She put the tortoiseshell spectacles on her nose and pulled out the little mirror. She stroked it, leaned it up against the glass, and suddenly the musicians inside played a cheery song, and the little mirror first showed her an outlandish landscape and then a bunch of tiny men who also sat around a table of green and white squares, covered in trays, bowls, saucepans, cups, glasses, and dishes filled with food. Blanca leaned toward Marta to look at the tiny men. They were pot-bellied dwarves, some with short dark hair, some bald, who wore gold chains around their necks and rings on their fingers. Marta took a first bite, groaned, and started blowing on the food. She drank water. The two chilly flies buzzed and flew from the window to Marta's plate, and she waved one hand to scare them off. The tiny men inside the little mirror were talking. They stirred their food with forks and spoons. This way and that. They said blah-blah-blah, they brought it to their mouths and chewed, still talking.

When Margarida returned to the house, she scolded Blanca as if she had never left. She told her, *Nasty, horrid girl!* and *Animal!*, because the women and the children had been living and sleeping and pissing and shitting all that time in the kitchen, *Like beasts, like brutes, like savages!* Margarida arrived with her eyes boiled like two eggs, carrying a serious infant with no name, and a permit from the viceroy to rebuild the house. She said, *Enough, that's it!* And everyone obeyed. She pointed at the beams, the black walls, the fireplace, the rubble, what was left of the stairs, the ripped-up beds, the weeds growing inside the house, the flies, the bugs, the rinds, the ash, the rotted esparto grass cushion. And Blanca, Bartomeu, and Esteve, following her orders, cleaned up and repaired the destruction. Even that taciturn and serious baby who didn't yet walk, whom Margarida called Guilla, because of his fox face, did what he was told. If his mother said, *Don't move,* he didn't move; *Don't cry,* he didn't cry. The only one who didn't obey was Joana. She just laughed. Margarida covered Joana's mouth, saying, *Sssh* because she didn't want anyone walking by to hear her and discover them, and Margarida threatened her, saying that if Joana wasn't silent, she'd gag her. Margarida glanced at Blanca's belly, which had swollen, and every once in a while asked her remorsefully, *What did they do to you? What did they do to you? Bad, bad men. Poor, poor little Blanca.* Blanca shrugged, but Margarida, who wasn't expecting a response, averred that no more men would enter that house. She ticked off a list: *Neither thieves, nor viceroy's men, nor coopers, nor farmhands, nor master wolfhunters, nor soldiers, nor suitors, nor peddlers, nor haulers, nor day laborers, nor purveyors, nor honorable travelers, nor vendors, nor merchants, nor charcoal burners, nor battle-scarred men, nor passersby! Enough. Not a single one. We're done.* She was so vehement, so angry, so imperious and imperative, that the house obeyed too. It shrunk down, hiding itself so it couldn't be found. And then, when Blanca and the children were weeding and hoeing the garden, Margarida would turn and scream at the hazelnut trees, the birch, the ash, the oak, the holm oak, the brambles, and the mallows, telling them to swallow up the hoed land, the terraces, the sheafs, the paths covered in rabbit droppings, the trails. Everything except that wreck of a house and that bit of garden. And at night they heard them, the obedient trees, how they crackled and embraced them, how they ate up the paths and shortcuts, how they grew thicker, narrower, and covered with thorns as they held hands. The valleys and the slopes crunched, at dawn, squeezing them. The ravines and the gullies sizzled. The springs and the torrents multiplied. The fog rose up whistling, each and every morning, and shrouded them with such attentiveness that often the sun would set without its cover vanishing. All together they kept the disgraced farmhouse and the women living inside it safe and so ardently hidden that not only did they soon fall into oblivion among the sparse inhabitants of the region, but so secreted away were they that even the passage of time eventually forgot the house, and the years overlooked it and the women inside. And thus, as many world events as one could possibly list took place over those many years, each and every one unheeded, twice over, by that farmhouse nestled in its burrow.

One of the dwarves inside Marta's little mirror got angry. He shouted and pointed at the tiny man beside him. All the other little men went eee and ooo, and stood up from the table. They raised their hands. The incensed dwarf started making threats, but they convinced him to keep the peace, and they went on eating and chewing. When they'd finished their meal, some miniature naked ladies showed up and began dancing. The tiny men watched them with gleaming eyes and teeth. Soon more small men came, with black eyebrows and fat fingers, but Marta touched the little mirror and the dwarves froze. With furious faces. Marta cleared the empty plate and glass. She stacked them in the sink and left the kitchen. Her footsteps sounded as she climbed the stairs; they stopped at Bernadeta's room, crossed the parlor, entered the bathroom, walked back down the stairs. She was whistling. Marta left the house every day at that same time. She bundled up and went outside. She got into a horseless carriage and departed.

Flies landed on the counter again. They no longer climbed on each other; now they were licking the splatters. Elisabet and Blanca strained the offal. They drained and fried it with chopped onion, parsley, and wine. And Blanca thought about how, when Margarida had said that no more thieves, no viceroy's men, no coopers, no farmhands, no master wolfhunters, no soldiers, no suitors, no peddlers, no haulers, no day laborers, no purveyors, no honorable travelers, no vendors, no merchants, no charcoal burners, no battle-scarred men, no passersby would enter this house, she hadn't said anything about not letting in martens or nasty women, or genets, weasels, or whores, or dim women, or dungheaps of vice, or doors through which the devil sneaks into men and makes them great sinners. And because of that, even though Margarida had shouted,

No, no, no! Let her give birth in the forest, let the foxes eat her baby!, when Blanca saw Elisabet on the threshing floor, like a little animal lost in the fog, she took her by the hand and brought her inside the house. Her fingers were freezing, and her belly was even more protuberant and fat than the one Blanca herself was lugging around. The two women were like a mirror. And from that day on, Blanca and Elisabet loved each other. In every possible way there is to love. Like the roe deer, delicately. Like the hens, obligingly. Like the ducks, with brute force. Like the goats, impatiently. Like the hares, playfully. Like the dogs, thirstily. Like the flies, furtively. Like the cats, ruthlessly. Like the foxes, friskily. Like the pigs, as if they'd loved each other for centuries.

AFTERNOON

En hitt veit eg eigi hvaðan þjófsaugu eru komin í ættir vorar.*
BRENNU-NJÁLS SAGA

The sky clouded over. Wispy fog arrived first, frayed, rapid, flying low. Then dark and heavy stacked clouds, dragging gusts and squalls, insect-devouring birds, and cornered insects. Dry leaves and branches flew off the ground as if trying to escape. A dense hood covered the peaks. And while the clouds huddled like a herd near the farmhouse, the sun stuck skinny orange fingers into the holes, and every time the clouds cut through them, the trees would shiver suddenly, as if they'd been shoved. The house, resigned and impassive, turned its back to the blackness gathering like a snorting herd on its roof.

In the kitchen, pots and pans burbled. The liquid on the gravy stew was blond and oily. On the lungs, it was toasted and thick. On the tripe, dark and speckled with parsley. The forcemeat was a light bubbling mass. Joana grabbed a spoon and tasted the stew.

---

* But I cannot imagine how thief's eyes have come into our kin.

She went, "Mmm, mmm, mmm!" as she passed the spoon to the other women so they could have a lick. Then she tasted the lungs and the tripe, and as she commended them she extinguished all the fires except for the one under the forcemeat, which she only stirred. She smiled with satisfaction, revealing her few teeth. They covered the fritters with a rag, and the pots with lids that didn't quite fit. One pot was squat, another blue with white dots, and a third was scarlet. Joana ordered Àngela to scrub the stove, the countertop, and the table, which were a jumble of peels, parings, and oil stains. She ordered Dolça to sweep. And Blanca and Elisabet to wash the dirty jars, plates, utensils, and silverware.

When Elisabet arrived at the farmhouse, she slept a sleep darker than if she'd been lying dead in a ditch. The Virgin, to whom she'd prayed to kill the miller from Roses and Clavell, had appeared amid the fog and taken her by the hand. Elisabet followed Her and allowed Her to tuck her beneath a blanket. The Mother of God did not speak, She just watched. She was also pregnant. And when Elisabet would wake up, She cared for her. She rubbed her feet. She brought them back to life, and Elisabet dozed off. When she awoke, she presented her ankles so She could touch them as if remaking them. She fell asleep again. And when she stirred, the caresses were traveling up her legs like ladybugs. Elisabet was dreaming, and by the time she began to awake, the tenderness had reached her knees. She dozed more, and halfway between reviving and lethargy, she moaned with her eyes closed to make sure that those savage, saintly hands found her. They were unlike any hands that Elisabet had known before, which had all belonged to men, and had always left splinters. Blanca's hands were both maternal and savage, both awkward and dexterous, both dirty and clean, mute and blind, too, and they were guided by touch, sighs, and warmth, and they didn't know which places another woman could touch you and which she couldn't. Elisabet groaned to encourage them, surreptitiously, at first masking her desire, ashamed, confused, and then eagerly, impatient for them to pounce on her barbarously and touch her everywhere. For them to wander over her thighs like hams, for them to grab her ass without hesitation, for them to touch her back and her hard belly, for them to clutch her breasts, and for them to nestle between her legs, there where it is always dark. Sometimes Elisabet would cry. Filled with water. Without speaking, because Blanca had no need for words. Blanca stretched out by Elisabet's side and drank her tears. The two stuffed bellies, a child inside each one, bumped. And when a tear slid past Elisabet's nose, on a trail that led to her lips, creeping into her mouth like an ant into an anthill, Blanca swallowed it just the same.

Elisabet opened first. With her gigantic, misshapen belly. The discomfort grew and flooded her. Her legs stiffened. The pain withdrew, and Blanca tickled her there where her arms folded. But the hurt came back, like the waves. Elisabet tried to find a place to grip, but the sea carried her off. She opened her eyes and saw nothing, she opened her mouth and only water flowed in. She felt her bones separating. She had seen a drowned man, once. With blue lips, chewed eyes, and a belly like hers, swollen. The sea swell passed. The water was cool, blue. Then it returned. It carried her to the depths and inundated her. Elisabet screamed, but water came out. She shrieked, but out came more water. She cried, and water flowed. Then the waves of pain retreated. Blanca scrubbed her back and legs. Elisabet gulped air and panted but the sea's beating was insistent, unbearable. She murmured, *No.* She whimpered, *No.* She shook her head. *No!* She stood up, clumsy and helpless, incapable of going anywhere. *No, I don't want to.* And Margarida, who was boiling bay leaves, wormwood, and yellow lily, heard her, and, filled with a poison that could also serve as a poultice, she called out to her, *For a baby to come out, its mother has to go through torture! All of us who are here, look at us! We were all born from inside our mothers! Every creature is born from inside its mother.*

Blanca did not move from her side. She thought about the sows who huffed and grunted, with a piglet's leg appearing between their haunches. Just the tip. Wet. And then the whole leg. The mothers wheezed, and the little ones twisted, and when one came out, soon another followed, yelp! and it was out. One butt-first and the other face-first. But the sow didn't get up, because there were more inside her, waiting. The nanny goats strolled with their bellies immense, hard, and round. They walked with their legs splayed and dripping with viscous, transparent liquid. Then they lay down, moaning and pushing, with their backsides bulging and the front legs of the kid sticking out of them like lances. The roe deer released a sticky juice and licked it. Their bellies rose and fell rapidly. They looked out into the void and pushed, they leaned their necks and they pushed. You could see the little head beneath the mother's small tail, which suddenly lifted. The fawn was hanging out of her. As if it were dead. Its head dark and wet and its front legs halfway out, swaying, still sleepy and covered in snot. The mother gnawed on grass, but eating didn't cure such intense pain, and she lay down again, and blood came out, and shit came out, and then the roe deer was born.

But Margarida had gotten herself worked up and was shouting, *I prayed for you to die.* She looked at Elisabet with eyes like awls. *Both of you. I prayed for them to kill you in terrible ways.* She pointed at her. *And if I let you give birth to that child of adultery, like a snake, here, it's only to give thanks.* She sighed loudly. *To thank God Almighty for not heeding my prayers, and for plugging up the devil's ears with wax. Because if you're alive, that means it wasn't my fault they killed Francesc.* But Elisabet wasn't listening to her; she was one big, red, slippery groan, just teeth, open mouth, pink lips between her legs, and a wilderness of hair, through which a green crown was coming into view, coming and coming, and when the head was out—just the head, with hair already—he was crying. With his purple mouth. And it seemed impossible that those screams could come out of such a little baby who hadn't even made it all the way out of his mother. When he did, he was still bellowing, and Margarida looked at him and said, *He's got the face of a thief.* But Elisabet took him in her arms, and she realized that she'd given birth to an infant ugly as a scowl. A frightened, scrawny creature, red and pimply, with a head like an egg, a wrinkled face, and little clawlike fingers, who didn't look like Clavell, because he was as ugly as if he had no father. Hideous as if he had no mother. Poor thing. And Elisabet consoled him, because she thought she had it in her to love an unsightly and gawky child.

Clavell had said that the child would be called Francesc, but Elisabet named him Martí. And the women called him Martí the Tenderhearted, because he always wanted his mother. He wanted Elisabet to lick his cuts and blow on his nettle stings, to kiss his skinned knees and sit him on her lap. He wanted Elisabet when he cried in sadness and when he cried from laughter, stretched out on the ground, his hands on his belly, his cheeks wet, his ears sticking out, and his gap-toothed mouth like a beak going, *Ay, ay, ay.* Clavell had also said that it was a barren farmhouse, sunken and rank, gripping the earth like a leech, but the musicians in Elisabet's head played a big concert, with all the cornemuses, the violins, the viola, the double bass, the clarinets, and a trumpet, and they even sang, when she gazed at the hidden house in the afternoons, when the sun fell and she bustled about in silence beside Blanca, or when Martí climbed up onto her lap and asked her to tell him the story of when he was born, again. Then the boy pointed at Àngela, and Elisabet pulled her close as well and cuddled her, because Blanca was like a cow who would forget about her calf. Martí asked her, *Is it true that we played together even when we were fish swimming in bellies?* Elisabet nodded, and she told them that when she and Blanca were pregnant, they would lie down side by side so they could play together, *like this, like this, elbowing and kicking.* And then Martí asked Elisabet to tell them how Àngela was born. Elisabet explained that even before Martí was all the way out in the world, he was already hollering, but when Àngela was born, she didn't cry. Martí added admiringly, *Because Àngela never cries.* Elisabet continued, *She was observing us! She stuck her head out between Blanca's legs, after a big rush of water, and looked around as if she were staring out a window. It can't be, we thought. Those eyes have only just opened, they've never seen anything! Just darkness inside the womb. The light now, it pierces and scratches.* Then she added that when Àngela's shoulders emerged, and then her body, white and blue, followed by more water, Margarida grabbed her by the feet, upside down like a rabbit, and smacked her bottom. Once. And again. And again. And again. But not even then did she cry. She gaped at them, serene, as if she'd enjoyed being born. As if she were pleased by the shoving and the cramming, the sudden light, the unveiled sounds, the scents no longer damp, the touch of dry things, the hands that grabbed her by the feet like a rabbit and smacked her upside-down bottom, over and over again.

The sound of a horseless carriage was heard, making the arrival path crackle. The main door opened and someone wiped their shoes before entering the farmhouse. The women turned. Blanca, Elisabet, and Àngela had finished washing and scrubbing, and now they were polishing the silverware and the blue-stemmed cups they would use for the party. Dolça was still sweeping. Everything they told her to do took a long time, because she was easily distracted. She was thinking about Filet, and all the things he'd said, and about Mr. Goodafternoon, and the kisses he gave her, and about Hurts Here, and then about Lleig and about Baby Jesus . . . , and the list never ended, because Dolça had had a string of lovers and beloveds so long that there was no end to it, and when she ticked them off she would lose track, and she would sweep the same spot she'd already swept thrice before, and step in the little mounds of debris she'd gathered, scattering them again.

Through the glass panes of the kitchen door, the women could see Alexandra coming into the house. Alexandra was Marta's daughter. A petite thing with drooping eyes, delicate features, skinny legs, and long hair, who made a face and covered her nose the moment she set foot in the entryway. She wore tight pants, a tiny blouse, and shoes that were too big, as if they had to accommodate bandaged-up feet. She climbed the stairs lugging a pink bag, and the women heard her walk across the parlor and enter the little room where Marta washed clothes. It was a small square space, with two white chests with round doors and crowded shelves. Alexandra bustled about. Her footsteps crossed back through the parlor and entered her room, which was by far the tidiest in the house. She had a full-length mirror, a desk, a chair, a bed, a pearl-colored rug, and a closet filled with neatly hung and folded clothes and shoes arranged just so. The walls were covered in the faces of saints without haloes, all very handsome and with shiny eyes and mouths open as if they were hungry. Then the footsteps upstairs left that room and peeked into Bernadeta's. They padded into the old woman's room, approached her bed, and a moment later they left and went down the stairs. The pink bag now looked full. Alexandra entered the kitchen and went, oof!, and waved her hand in front of her nose. But the women had left the things they were doing half-done and they'd drawn close to the window, Dolça leading the way. They craned their necks and looked outside. On the threshing floor there was a horseless carriage, and inside it was a young man. They heard Alexandra rummaging around in the pantry. She lit the light, opened the well of ice, sighed, and shut it. She went back to the kitchen, over to the swan's mouth, the women shifted aside to make way, and she filled a glass with water, which she set on the counter. The young woman pulled out the little mirror, brought it to her mouth and said, in a severe but indolent voice, Mama, I can't find my white sneakers, do you know where they are?, Great-Grandma is sleeping and I made sure not to wake her up, we're going to Olot now, mwah. Then she took a sip of water, and before leaving the house, she rinsed the cup. The women, prying, watched through the window as she walked toward the horseless carriage, as she put the bag in the back and got inside, as she kissed the young man curled up there on the mouth. They couldn't see his face clearly, but from the form of his nape, his back, and his chestnut-brown hair, Dolça, who'd been studying him for a while, thought he looked like her Flabiol. She'd called that lover Flabiol because he played the pan flute. He was handsome, and he practiced while hidden like a secret in forest clearings. He had shiny hair, stiff and slicked back, and a kissy-kissy mouth that didn't know how to be still. When his kissy-kissy mouth wasn't playing the pan flute, it was kissing, and when it wasn't kissing, it whispered that in going from one local festival to another, and from one Sunday dance to the next, he would find nymphs hidden in the forest! Flabiol's father had taught him about music but never played in front of people who weren't his own kids. Luckily, he had a ton of kids. Ten children, including two sets of twins, because, as Flabiol would say, his mother just needed to glance at his father's underwear and she'd be pregnant. And Flabiol's father, realizing how Flabiol studied him when he played for his kids, had gifted him a shepherd's pan-pipe, in two pieces and with a reed made of jujube wood. Flabiol explained to Dolça that, when he first started playing, he would earn ten or eleven silver pieces, plus the cost of traveling here and there and everywhere, but that later, little by little, he made more money from music than from working the forest. He smiled con-tentedly, his chest puffed up and his eyes mischievous, and he smelled clean, as if he'd been washed and ironed before leaving the house, and he added, *I shouldn't say this, but I know more than two hundred songs by heart! And as self-taught musicians go, I'm one of the best.* And then he would grab her tight and tickle her as he pleaded, *Nymph, faerie, water sprite, please let me go back home!*, as if Dolça were a nymph who had trapped him in the for-est, *the queen of all the faeries!*, and she would laugh like a vain-glorious hen.

The horseless carriage, which emitted shrill music, made two spirited and unnerving circles in front of the house. Pressed up against the window, the women watched the spectacle. The arms of the couple dangled out either side of the carriage. And then they left, just as they'd come. Àngela was the only one who didn't watch them.

Martí's eyes would flick open like a frog's when Àngela jumped. From the little balcony off the parlor. He would raise his hands to his head, and Àngela would throw herself into the void like a bird without wings. She would fall onto the threshing floor and break both her legs. But she would hardly limp. *Does it hurt?* Martí would ask, kneeling beside her to blow on her scratches and bloody wounds, the slashes where he could see bone, the swellings, the lumps, the nettle stings, the dislocated shoulders with dangling elbows, the swollen bruises, the blisters, the burns. And he would kiss her, the way his mother once kissed him. Àngela felt no pain, but she felt the kisses. And she was always walking around with her arms and legs black and blue, yellow, green, purple, and all the colors of bruises. Until Margarida would catch her with that purple belly and back, with her thighs gray like a blue girl's, with her hands destroyed from picking up embers, with those two fuchsia arms like two skies at sunset, and she would shout, *Rootless ingrates, wound-salters, wretches!* as she dragged Martí off by one ear and whipped him. She didn't beat Àngela, because what was the point. She healed her and sometimes she tied her up, so she wouldn't walk on broken legs. And she forbade them from seeing each other, as a punishment. Then she ordered her son Guilla, *Keep an eye on them.* She repeated many times, *Don't leave the house.* Guilla, who was a pensive, cautious, and mature child with a round face, a small mouth, and ash blond hair, kept an eye on them, and he taught them to forage golden chanterelles, to extract pine nuts from pine cones, to fish for barbels, to find wild strawberries, garlic and onions, downy birch sap, rosemary, red clover, ladder snakes, dandelions, blackberries, asparagus, acorns, chestnuts, figs, and arbutus berries, without ever losing sight of the farmhouse among the trees. He had them gather broom branches, since they burn best. Fennel for making omelets that make you strong. Nettles for steeping infusions that make you robust. Àngela and Martí were fond of Guilla because he was like a father who was a child. He would tell them, *Look for the blackcaps and the hidden nests they make with thin branches in the scrub.* He would point to the full moon and murmur, *You see the eyes? You see the mouth?* Martí would whisper, *It's crying,* but Guilla would say, *It's singing!* Because Guilla knew things and Guilla had seen people, with those solemn gray eyes of his, he had met people who weren't Joana, or Margarida, or Blanca, or Elisabet, or Bartomeu, or Esteve, when he'd been in prison with his mother. Àngela and Martí had never seen anyone but those who lived in that farmhouse. They'd never been to a town or a market. And they listened to him in terror. There were many men, and many women. *How many?* He couldn't remember anymore. *More than the birds and more than the bees,* he told them. And sometimes Martí would cry from the anguish that thought provoked in him. When they found a dead fox or a baby bird fallen from its nest, with its belly too swollen and its head too big, just beak and eyes covered in worms, Guilla would make them look at it. Because this was death, he would explain. And sometimes they would play dying. All three of them. They would run and shriek, *They're coming! They're coming!* and *They found us! They found us!,* and they'd fall to the ground and groan because thieves and soldiers and wolves and evildoers and people from the towns and from the cities were coming and would find them and eat them and kill them. Bartomeu and Esteve didn't want to play. They said it was a game for little kids and that they were nearly grown. That they had other work to do. Margarida would tell them to bring Joana to the garden. And they had to lift up her skirt and hear her piss and shit. And sometimes she splattered them. Other times they took her out and she didn't do anything, and then they'd bring her back to the house and she did all her business there, and Margarida would scold them because she'd have to clean the bench and the whole house stank. Bartomeu was strapping, with a thick neck, dark hair, and shiny, fleshy lips. Esteve was skinny, with a long neck, fair hair, and a mouth contorted into a permanent chuckle. His one ear stuck out. They went everywhere together like finger and nail, and they were only having fun with the little ones when they said, *Come on, Martí*, and they would take Martí into one corner to explain to him what *misbegotten* and *illegitimate* meant, and *bastard* and *lowborn*. Or when they went into the woods and made the littler ones stare at a low, narrow crevice in a rock wall where they swore the devil slept. A fusty smell came out of it, the scent of rotten leaves and ferret den. Bartomeu and Esteve went, *Sssh*, and the little ones listened. The forest crackled and the children's eyes grew small. They could almost see him, the He-Goat of Biterna, inside that dark slit, and then the older ones would shout, *Here he comes!*, and Martí, Àngela, and Guilla would run, and Bartomeu and Esteve would crack up laughing. Or when they wanted to play mommies and daddies, and the mommies and daddies wanted to have children. But they always fought. Because they both wanted to be the man, and neither of them wanted to be the woman. Bartomeu was stronger and he would win. And then he was the father and Esteve was the mother. Bartomeu would go off and the others had to wait for him to return. But when the children were left alone with Esteve and they called him Mom, he would say he wasn't their mother, that he was leaving so he wouldn't have to be their mother, and they'd be scared, cold, and hungry, and even though they'd beg, *Please, Mommy, don't leave*, he would abandon them just the same. And when he would chase them, and when he caught them, he'd beat them. Because they were bad children. Until Bartomeu came back and said he'd been to war and fought against the French. And Esteve complained that he was fed up, that he wanted to go to war, too, and fight against the French or against whomever. And the two boys were exasperated because in that hidden farmhouse they were missing the most important battles of the era. And they exclaimed that in that smelly house, instead of becoming men, they would stay little kids forever, because their mother bossed them around, do this and do that, as if they were still toddlers, and she scolded them, and she reprimanded them, and she even hit them when they knelt, with the two younger boys, around Àngela.

The girl was stretched out in the middle of the circle. Guilla and Martí were tickling her. They twisted her tender skin, which turned first white and red, and then sometimes blue, sometimes violet, and sometimes yellow with purple dots. They asked her, *Does this hurt?*, but it didn't, *What about here?*, but it didn't, *And this?* And then Bartomeu and Esteve said, *We want to play too*, and they knelt down. First they made little pinches. Laughing. Then bigger pinches. And when they saw that Àngela didn't yank her arms and legs away, they sank their nails into her and made her bleed. But Àngela didn't complain. And then they hit her. With their fists. But the girl didn't cry, and then they grabbed her fingers and bent them backward. But she didn't scream. And Bartomeu and Esteve got angry because she looked at them impassively from the ground, with cunning and tranquil eyes, not batting a lash. And they went to find sticks and rocks to make her bleed even more, and once they were standing they kicked her in the mouth, in the belly, and in the back, because they were furious. Martí and Guilla shouted, *Don't kill her, don't kill her! Please!*, and Àngela's head went this way and that, and all she saw was red, orange, and black. And then she saw nothing at all. Martí and Guilla told her that when Margarida heard her shrieks and found them, she hit Bartomeu and Esteve so hard that *they* cried. And when Àngela woke up, she still couldn't open her eyes, because they were so swollen, and she could eat only with great effort, and Bartomeu and Esteve were no longer there, because they'd gone off forevermore to be soldiers.

The sound of another horseless carriage was heard, making

the path crunch. Soon after, the front door opened and someone shouted, hellooo! Hellooo! Hellooo! Uproarious. As if they wanted the stones inside the walls to know they'd arrived. The women, who were again polishing silver and cups, looked through the panes of the kitchen door and observed a mother and two kids taking off their jackets and unloading backpacks and bags. A short little girl with a pointed voice said she wanted to see the baby goat. She had hair that covered her eyebrows, and her mouth was filled with silver. All her teeth were silver-plated and bound to one another. Rosa, who often came to the farmhouse in the after-noons, told the girl that first she had to say hi to Bernadeta. Rosa's head was small and long, her shoulders rounded, her breasts perched way up high, her hair curly, and her eyebrows so pale she had to draw them on. The girl rummaged around inside a white bag and pulled out a box. With her silvery mouth she asked, are these the only ones you bought? The woman said yes, and the little girl said that she wanted different cookies. The boy, who also had a silver mouth but was taller, laughed, and his sister said to him, shut up, Nico.

They went upstairs. The noise must have awakened Bernadeta, because greetings could be heard from below. Then a ruckus of feet coming down the staircase. Rosa shouted, Sheila, slow down! and the girl answered, without stopping, that she was going to see the baby goat in the pens. The boy, nearly a teen, walked be-hind her. He went into the kitchen and all the women looked at him. He had long eyelashes, dark eyes, skin covered with red and white spots. He ran his eyes over the walls, the sink, the window, the table, the fireplace. He sighed and dropped into a chair at the head of the table, where Marta had eaten her lunch. He pulled out a little mirror and stroked its brilliance, his strokes making high-pitched sounds until a pixie appeared. The pixie went down a mountain and gathered coins from the air. Nico watched it, focused, and moved his fingers quickly, skillfully, until the pixie fell and the little mirror went clong!, and Nico snorted as if he were angry. Dolça, who was still sweeping, pushed her hair back behind her ears, because it wasn't often that young men were in that house. And this was the second one today! He had pretty lips, this young man did, and Dolça swept between his legs to get a better look at them. And she wondered if those lips surrounded by peach fuzz already knew how to kiss, or if they were ashamed, like Manta, who would turn red and say, *Not so close*, if Dolça drew too near. His name was Isidre, but Dolça called him Manta because when she'd found him, he had been sleeping, quiet and still, stretched out on a folding lounge chair and covered with a blanket. He had a yellow face and pink lips. And Dolça had watched him for a long time, because she had never been able to look at a young man up close before. Until Manta awoke and said, *What are you doing?!* and Dolça replied, *What are you doing?"* He was sunbathing, because he was ill. He had a delicate voice, and explained that the mountain was no longer good for tourism, because they'd let the hotel get flattened during the war. *And you've got all these springs*, he said. And he told her about the cow. Dolça liked the story of the cow. Once upon a time there was a cow who pissed blood. But when the animal grazed through those woods, and drank water from those peppery springs, her urine turned lighter and she was cured. And that was how first the farmers, and then the doctors, discovered that the water here was good for healing the sick.

If Dolça drew too close to look at his pretty, girlish lips, his little chin, and his big nose and mouth, as if his face had shrunk from his illness, Manta would get embarrassed, and he'd say, *Not so close, I'm vulnerable.* But if Dolça asked him, *Can I hold your hand?,*

Manta would let his hand drop off the lounge chair. He smelled of medicine. And Dolça would sit by his side and place his hand on her head. Playfully. She would lower it over her forehead, gradually. Over her eyelids and her eyelashes and then over her nose and mouth, chin and neck. She brought it to her nape, and her back, beneath her clothes, to the tips of her shoulders, first one, then the other, and then to her front, to her breasts, where his hand tensed up, but didn't pull away.

Sheila ran into the kitchen and said that the baby goat wasn't in the pens. She asked her brother if he wanted to go investigate, and Nico, without looking at her, said that he was playing. The girl spun around and went back to the entryway. The women saw how she opened the built-in cabinet, how she peeked inside and closed the door, and how she touched the milk pitchers. She tried to pick them up. She looked at the wicker molds and the cheese lyre that hung on the walls. She shrugged and went back to the kitchen, lugging the white bag and a red sack with handles and buckles. From the bag she pulled out a bottle and a box of cookies, and her brother, his eyes fixed on the pixie going down the mountain gathering coins, said he wanted a snack too. The girl leaned on the counter, jumped up to open the doors to all the cabinets, and took out two cups. She poured herself an orangish liquid, sat down on the bench and opened the box of cookies, bit into one, sighed loudly, and again grumbled that she wanted different ones. She drank and asked Nico if he had any homework. The boy made a sound that was neither a yes nor a no. Then he added that his class was going on a field trip the next day. The pixie went tlling, tlling every time he got a coin, and clong! every time he fell. The girl asked, a field trip where? and Nico, as if answering required great effort, said that they were going kayaking on the reservoir. Sheila exclaimed, lucky ducks! and she opened up the red sack. She pulled out two bundles of paper and a small bag with writing tools, which she scattered over the table. Then she added, this house stinks, and her brother laughed. Àngela turned her back on them.

Sometimes Martí and Àngela wanted to play with Guilla, but other times they preferred to play alone. And they would hide. Àngela would ask him, *How?* and Martí would say, *Like tickles, like caresses, but on the flip side. But how? Like piercing, like cutting, like burning.* But Àngela didn't understand. *Are you hurting me?* she would ask. Martí said, *Yes* but no. *What about this? No. What do you feel?* She felt the weight, the roughness of his little animal fingers, the rubbing, the cadence, the eager blood, Martí's hands on her body, Martí's mouth, so close to her ears, saying, *You have a stone, Where?, Here.* There was no light with which to see it. Only fingers. Martí's hands on Àngela's flat chest. On her small nipples. *Here.* They felt them. There were two. One on either side. And then the stones grew. Very slowly. The two children would hide and rub them. From two small stones like two wild strawberries, they became two small stones like two acorns. From two acorns, two chestnuts. From two chestnuts, two walnuts. From two walnuts, two small apples. Martí grasped hold of them and Àngela opened her mouth like a fish out of water. And then they were no longer interested in pain, but in tickling, in thirst, in folds, in shivers, in crannies, in panting, in holes, the one for making pee-pee, the one for making big turds, and the third one that only Àngela had, where blood sometimes came out, but Martí didn't ask if it hurt, because he already knew it didn't.

Until one day of the many days when Margarida caught them, hidden, on top of each other, and shouted, *You'll go to hell! Like animals, like dogs, like cats. Nasty! Always thick as thieves!*, and when they replied, *Hell has to be better than this farmhouse*, and when

Margarida answered, *You'll go to hell, and in hell they'll separate you*, Guilla said, *Let them marry.* And the idea of them marrying fell to the ground like a pine nut, and sprouted, and made a pine tree covered in pine cones filled with pine nuts. And then everyone wanted to have a wedding. A real party, because no one could remember the last time they'd thrown a party in that hibernating house. And even though Margarida said that wasn't really getting married, they grabbed eggs from every nest they could find, and Guilla hunted three partridges. They plucked them, and they stuffed them with hard-boiled eggs, mint, parsley, garlic, sage, rosemary, and dried figs, and with the partridges' own hearts and their own fried kidneys. And then they cooked them on a spit, and while they roasted, they smeared them with a paste made of pine nuts and egg yolks. And they even made another sauce with the livers, the broth from boiling the necks and the tips of the wings, which are greasy, and with more crushed pine nuts, which released white milk. And when the time came for the party to start, Guilla bound Martí and Àngela's wrists, and they went this way and that with their hands knotted together, feeding each other, and parading their love around with closed eyes, and their blood boiled inside them, oily and sweetened. Guilla sang. Blanca clapped. Joana danced, using just a little arm and a little leg. Elisabet cried. And Àngela, who understood very little about tears, because she herself had never cried, thought they were tears of joy, but really they were tears of pain.

That night, Elisabet lay down, all white and trembling, getting up only to vomit. Then she vomited lying down. Joana spat streams of slaver, and with her tongue rigid she cried, *Thyme! Thyme! Give her thyme.* No one understood her until she'd said it thirty times over. Blanca gave mugs and mugs of thyme to the patient. When she couldn't swallow, she applied it to her lips with a rag. The woman was pissing blood, and Martí begged her, *Please don't die, please don't die, Mother.* But Elisabet's back grew more and more drenched, as if she were swimming in a pool. Her hair stuck to her forehead, the flesh of her cheeks to her bones, and she was panting. She looked at Blanca and in a thin hiss of a voice she whispered, *Thank you. Thank you. Thank you.* She gazed at Martí and murmured, *Thank you. Thank you. Thank you.* But Àngela didn't understand what she was giving thanks for. After that she spoke no more, she opened her mouth, her neck stiffened, her lips curled. They revealed her yellow, shrunken tongue, and her eyes grew small. They rolled backward, ambushed. And her hands coiled like ferns. Martí, by her side, held them and unfurled them. He kept repeating, *Please don't die, please don't die, Mother.* And when Elisabet died, Martí cried. He cried and cried and cried. All the time. Every day. Because he was used to Elisabet always doing what he asked. And he just wanted his mommy. Like when he was little. He would say to Àngela, *You don't understand* and he would whimper, *I've got sand, there's sand here,* pointing to his chest. And if he moved, the sand hurt him, and if he stretched out, the sand choked him. And Àngela really didn't understand how grief could possibly last so long.

EVENING

. . . many things get forgiven in the course
of a life: nothing is finished or unchangeable
except death and even death will bend a little if
what you tell of it is told right.

ALI SMITH, *HOW TO BE BOTH*

The light that entered through the window was lavender, and darkened the things inside the kitchen, each attended by its own shadow. The fritters, the gravy stew, the kid's lungs and intestine rested beneath cloths and lids. The women turned off the flame under the forcemeat and left it resting on the stove. Then they filled the sink with water, and Joana, Blanca, Elisabet, and Dolça stripped from the waist up, rolling, untying, and unbuttoning their clothes, and opening the tops of their dresses and blouses. With their breasts exposed, they ran a damp rag over their armpits, bellies, necks, and backs. Sheila and Nico were sitting at the table, heads bowed in concentration, ignoring the women's bathing. Joana's back was curved, stooped, covered in brown and purple splotches, red freckles, and warts. Blanca had round, soft, milky shoulders, her flesh slid down to her waist like cream. Elisabet had a long back, tanned and skinny, and her shoulder blades stuck out like wings. Dolça's back was short, with a well-defined spine and downy hair that came down in a dark line from her nape to her tailbone. Hurts Here would say to her, *Lie down,* and Dolça would lie down. He would say to her, *Where does it hurt?,* and Dolça would reply, *It hurts here . . .* or *It hurts there . . .* and Hurts Here would uncover the place she pointed to. They played the game of It Hurts Here and It Hurts There, and he would make believe he was operating on her with kisses, caresses, and his infallible tool, which was crooked but very healing. Hurts Here was a potbellied, joyful man, with a mustache and a double chin and a kind voice, who cured the sick in exchange for a bit of food and a bed to sleep in. He would always tell Dolça about the time he'd operated on that eight-year-old boy on a kitchen table, by the light of a carbide lamp, and saved his life. And there was the time he'd taken a tumor out of the neck of a mother in Osor, with a thin knife, grain alcohol, and a lamp surrounded by mirrors. In the middle of the operation, he'd run out of silk thread, and her husband had had to go out to find more. It was night-time, and he'd been able to find only pink thread, and Hurts Here used the pink thread and also saved that woman.

Àngela was hunchbacked, with a hump that stuck out like a pumpkin and lifted one of her shoulders higher than the other. She didn't take off her clothes and she didn't wash. When Àngela's belly swelled up, Margarida blurted out, *You're with child* and kept her eyes on her, because she was mumbling that the baby would fall out of her and onto the ground and Àngela wouldn't even notice. Actually, she did notice. Because she felt the urge to push. Not pain. Just the urge to evacuate. Like making a bowel movement. Constricted. And Margarida ordered, *Stay still, don't push, you'll tear*, but Àngela didn't care about tearing. Margarida had said, *A woman's greatest blessing is having babies*, but Àngela didn't feel lucky, giving birth to wads of soft bones and spongy flesh, infants who couldn't do anything for themselves and hogged up all of Martí's kisses. They named their first son after his father, and to differentiate him they called him Martí the Lame, because he was born with one leg shorter than the other. But even though Margarida screamed that all of them in that house were doomed, when the boy started walking, he limped no more than Àngela. They named the second child Bernadeta. And Margarida exclaimed, *She's just like her father*, because the baby cried all the time. She'd been born without eyelashes, and the women thought that happens sometimes, some babies are born without eyelashes and they grow in later, but Bernadeta's never did. And her eyes would fill with dust, with sand, with hair, with lint, with flies and junk, and they stung, and they itched, and the girl howled, shrieked, and yelled all day long, her face red and her voice hoarse, her eyes saddled with discharge hard as croutons. Margarida would come over and mumble what she'd heard Joana say: *God and the Virgin Mary, and Reverend Saint Peter, and Reverend Saint John, when traveling the road anon, a gallant wolf they do happen upon. Tell us, gallant wolf, whence are thou headed? To feast on the flesh and the blood of that infant!* But from her bench, spitting drool, Joana shook her head and screeched, *Thyme! Thyme! Give her thyme!* And when they understood her, after she'd said it thirty times over, Margarida murmured, *Thyme, again?* like a morbid joke.

At first it seemed that all those herbal infusions they poured into her eyes were making Bernadeta go quiet. But then her gaze turned yellow, and she opened her bald lizard lids wide. She looked into the void and shrieked as much as or worse than before.

Frightened. Alienated. Like a child unhinged. When she began to articulate words, she would just shout, *Father, father!* And soon came the unbearable questions. *Why are they cutting his ears?* she would ask. *Why doesn't he have a hole back there, the boy with no hole back there? Why are they poisoning the jenny?* Àngela would get exasperated: *Which jenny?! The jenny they left there, with her mouth and eyes open, and at first the wolves wouldn't even come near, but in the end they were hungry and they ate her, and then their bones danced, and they spat dripping white saliva, and their skin, under their fur, was blue. Then they died. All the wolves scattered. And then all the other animals died. The ones who'd tasted the jenny, and the ones who'd eaten any animal who'd tasted the jenny.* Àngela hushed her: *You're dreaming* and *Shush*, but Bernadeta would still talk, then about a faceless woman. Bernadeta asked if she was alive or dead when the wolves ate her nose and mouth, and Àngela screamed, *Stop making things up!* But Bernadeta continued insufferably, saying there was a man who had the runs, who crouched down bare-assed in a patch of forest, with such urgency and such bad luck that he let loose his shit on a nest of vipers. It wasn't until the nth time she told the story that she added that the man with the runs was hunting wolves, and that when he was an infant, the beasts had eaten all his siblings and the pinkie toe on his left foot. Then Margarida lifted Bernadeta off the ground and shook her. She frantically demanded to know whether the vipers had stung the man with no left pinkie toe, and the very insolent child had replied yes, but every time she tried to say where they'd stung him, she was overcome by a fit of laughter. Bernadeta stopped guffawing only when Martí the Tenderhearted came into the kitchen. Then she would stifle her laughter and shriek, *I don't want them to kill you, Father, I don't want them to kill you! I don't want the foxes to come eat you.*

Sheila lifted her head from the bundles of paper she had on the table and asked her brother if he knew what the troposphere was. Nico didn't answer, and the girl asked him again if he knew what the troposphere was. He said no, and Sheila said that she did, and then she asked, do you know what the stratosphere is? And Nico said no. And Sheila said that she did, and the mesosphere and the ionosphere? and Nico said that he used to know, but he forgot. And then Sheila asked if he knew what the exosphere was and he said no, stop being so annoying, and the girl answered that she didn't know either and that's why she was asking him. It started to rain. At first the drops were very spaced out. Heavy. One on this leaf, and the leaf swayed. One on that roof tile. And the roof tile pinged. And then they fell faster. Inside the house the convivial clamor of water was heard. The women got dressed, they ran their fingers through their hair, and then they sat around the table. Elisabet and Blanca on the long bench with Sheila. Joana in her corner in front of Nico. Dolça in a chair beside Àngela. They had everything ready, and all that was left was the waiting. But Àngela sighed loudly because they'd been waiting all day.

Even though Martí the Lame was the eldest, Bernadeta always made him cry. Because she was a lying, twisted, spiteful brat, and envious of her brother. Àngela would hit her, but she kept telling her terrible stories. And Martí the Lame, who had a round head, dark eyes, red ears, and widely spaced teeth, would listen good-naturedly and attentively, like when his father was a boy and hung on Bartomeu's and Esteve's words. Bernadeta would tell him that once upon a time a man and two boys went into a farmhouse and killed the owner, his wife, his daughter, the servant, and the maid, with knives they drove into their hands, chests, and stomachs. And when the law caught up to them, they were hanged. But the story didn't end there. They cut the hanged men into pieces. They separated their heads and legs and arms, and they put them up in the trees, jumbled, inside forged iron cages. And then came crows, swallows, sparrows, flies, wasps, and bumblebees, and they emptied out their eyes and they ate their flesh until you could see their skulls. And no matter how hard Àngela beat her, Bernadeta had an endless supply of stories of men who were hanged or who were lashed in public squares, and then their ears or the flesh of their loins was ripped off with pincers, and last of all, they were chopped into pieces. Stories of women who screamed and twisted as they were ravished. Scabrous and detailed fables of wolves that ate children who could feel each and every bite. And, as if Bernadeta weren't satisfied with having her brother constantly terrified and cringing, she would then tell him, *They'll kill you.* Martí the Lame looked at her with sensitive and desolate little eyes. *They'll make a hole in you here, and here, and so much blood will come out of you.* She pointed to his head and his chest, and when the poor thing, through his tears, asked her, *And how will they kill you?*, Bernadeta would reply, smiling, *They won't kill me. I will die of old age, in my bed, dreaming.*

Which was why Àngela asked Bernadeta, *Where are they?* when Martí the Tenderhearted, Guilla, and Martí the Lame went out to chop wood and hadn't come back. And when Àngela saw Bernadeta's treacherous, puffy face, with her eyes swollen from so much furtive sobbing, she asked her, *What do you know?* Bernadeta was now a woman, but she was just as twisted and burdensome, envious and spiteful as when she was a little girl telling her terrible stories, and at first she didn't want to say. Àngela insisted, *You must tell me.* But Bernadeta only moaned, *Mother, Mother, no, please . . .* , until her mother twisted her arms so hard that Bernadeta said that her father, her brother, and her uncle had been chopping wood when they came across two men in the forest. *One was old and the other was young. Their eyes were full of terror and their expressions incoherent. They seemed scared to death.* She explained that the strangers had been running through the forest and up the mountain for days. *When they discovered them, the young man got down on his knees. He lifted his hands and pleaded.* Bernadeta stuffed Àngela's apron into her own mouth, and Àngela yanked it out, as if she were tearing out her words. She murmured that she saw how those two strangers had fled, through houses, empty streets, and churches, because a group of men with red berets had entered their city and chased them. She mumbled that those who were escaping en masse didn't seem like soldiers, but rather simple men, unarmed, cowardly, who ran into the woods, and when they came upon a farmhouse that would give them three wineskins and a basket of apples, they sat down and rested. But one of them got up suddenly, and once again they ran with their mouths open, screaming in fear and pain because the men with the red berets had found them. Bernadeta said that some of them didn't even have the energy to stand up, and they just sat there and let themselves be killed. Those who could sought refuge by jumping over partitions, sheltered by the rocks, crossing terraced land, and escaping into the forest. And these two men, the old man and the young man, hid in a deep gully, and when night fell, wrapping them in a thick fog, they continued walking. In the dark, their clothing wet and snagging on the hawthorns, they found a path that led them into the thick of the woods, and at some point in the morning they sat down because the old man was very tired. And that was how the men from Mas Clavell came upon them. The young man who had dropped to his knees when he realized that the Martís and Guilla weren't the men with the red berets, begged them for help. Àngela was listening to Bernadeta and trying to imagine in detail the things she was describing. How Guilla and the two Martís had offered to lead them. How the old man lifted his arms to the sky and could barely stand up straight. The two Martís assisted him. But Bernadeta didn't want to continue. Àngela was of a mind to strangle her. She stopped thrashing Bernadeta only when she spoke again: *When the men with the red berets found them, Father tried to reason with them but they didn't listen. Father waved no with his hands, but they took them anyway.* Àngela heard a whistle. Weak but shrill. She was pinching Bernadeta, and Bernadeta whispered, *They tied them up two by two. The young man to Martí's back. Father to Uncle Guilla. The old man could no longer walk, and they stretched him out on the ground and crushed his head with a rock. And they took them to find more men with berets and more pleading prisoners.* The whistle was coming from Àngela's chest as she breathed. *They lined them up. And one birdlike man, dressed all in black, came over and forced them to kneel. Martí obeyed. The young man pulled out some coins and gave them to the black bird. Uncle Guilla closed his eyes. Father, with his hands tied, shook his head no. But they started shooting. First at a pair of men who were crying. Then at Father and Uncle.* The whistle in Àngela's chest sounded out louder and louder. *They fell to the ground, one on top of the other, with white faces, open mouths, and their blood mixing together.* Àngela wasn't crying, because she didn't know how to cry. She was whistling. And the whistle broke only when she demanded, *What else?! Then they shot Martí, tied to the young man's back, and they fell together. Martí beneath the young man. But Martí didn't die. He remained very still, on the ground, wet with blood, until they came by to check, and when some boots were stopped beside them, the body of the young man tied to Martí spasmed. And then they shot them again. In the head and in the chest.* Àngela touched her head and her chest. *Here, and here*, the way Bernadeta used to tell him they would kill him, when they were little. And Àngela asked, *What else?!* Bernadeta was whimpering. *What else?! Then they stripped off their clothes and they piled them up. What else?!* Àngela didn't feel the stabbing pain. *What else?!* And she wanted to feel it. *What else?!* She wanted to experience the torment, the piercing pain one must feel when so many of your loved ones are killed. *What else?!* She wanted to feel the torn, oozing gash. The knife inside, turning. Bernadeta's fingers inside, turning. She wanted her mouth to open in a grimace, her lips to curl and reveal her red gums. *Then the foxes came. What else?!* Her tongue to shrink into the depths of her throat, her eyes to fall inward, and her hands to coil like ferns, and for Martí to have to open them. And to be able to tell him, I understand now, I understand now, Martí.

Sheila wasn't writing anymore; she was drawing. She was sketching girls with big eyes and big breasts and little noses, and boys with broad shoulders and hair falling across their features. Nico was still busy with his mirror. Joana looked around the purple kitchen at the bored, respectable faces that filled it, and it seemed to her that the dusky light and the stillness of the waiting were dampening their mood and the spirit of the party. And to make the time pass a little faster, she said:

"Once upon a time there was an old man, very old, and poor, who had only one donkey and three lazy sons, and one day he went to bed and never got out of it again. The man thought, I'm old. Any day now I'll close my eyes and never open them again, and I have to figure out what to do with my donkey. He gathered his children around his bed and told them, *My sons, I am old and any day now I shall die. Head out into the world and return in one year's time, at which point whichever son of mine has done the laziest deed shall be the one to whom I leave the donkey after my demise.*"

The two sweet-toothed flies hovered over Sheila's glass of juice. The girl scared them off. Joana continued:

"The older brother and the middle brother headed out into the world, but the little one didn't. When the year was up, the two brothers returned home, went over to the bed where their father lay wasting away, and the eldest said, *Father, the donkey is mine.* The ailing father asked, *What have you done? Tell me! It was summer,* said the eldest brother. *I was swimming in a river basin, when suddenly I felt so lazy that I couldn't move my arms nor my legs. I was drowning, but I didn't exit the water, out of pure sloth. Luckily, some people saw me and pulled me out, half-dead.* But the second brother exclaimed, *Father, the donkey is mine. I'm lazier than my older brother. Explain,* said the old man. *It was winter, a freezing-cold night, and I was sitting by the fireplace of a house I'd arrived at that evening. An ember leapt from the fire and landed on my foot, but out of laziness and contentment, I didn't shake it off. I did want it off my foot, because it was causing me intense pain, but my laziness was stronger. Until the people in the house, smelling the scent of charred flesh, removed it.* The little brother didn't say anything. *And what about you, my son, what have you done?* asked his father. The boy yawned and said, *I won't answer that, Father, I'm too lazy to even put a few words together.* He yawned again, even wider, and the donkey was his. A few days later, their father died, and they were so lazy they didn't even bury him."

Joana burst out into a braying cackle, and the women joined in. They clapped and stomped their feet and cheered. The kids and the flies didn't flinch. Dolça got up onto a chair and whistled with her fingers in her mouth. The Bad Hunter had taught her to whistle. He had a different whistle for everything, and his dogs knew what each meant. He'd showed Dolça how to position her lips, *like a kiss*, and then how to place her fingers inside her mouth, *like that, very good.* And suddenly he would go, *I finally caught the hare!* and he'd carry her on his shoulders as if she were a trophy. The Bad Hunter was a small, good-looking man. Strapping, with a thick back, neck, and chest, and red hair and a mustache. He had tiny fair eyes that hid beneath his brows like two caves, his ass was like an apple, and his jaw was like a well-closed drawer. Dolça called him the Bad Hunter because, instead of hunting, he would lie with her, nestled among a hot carpet of happy backs, heads, snouts, and tails. Then Dolça stroked his mustache, because the Bad Hunter liked to have his mustache caressed, and he would tell her about the high-pitched bark his dogs made when they'd located their prey. He taught her how to whistle, and the dogs pricked up their ears.

Rosa entered the kitchen amid the women's racket. She exclaimed, it's too dark to see! and she turned on a light, which flickered aggressively. Dolça came down from the chair, as if she'd been caught being naughty. Rosa touched Sheila's head and Nico's cheek and said, that's enough playing, time to stop. But Nico ignored her. His mother put a mug inside the urn and said that Bernadeta's mouth was dry and she didn't want supper, but she wanted cookies and some chamomile tea to wash them down with. Sheila went on drawing. The mug spun around. The two flies landed on the counter in front of Rosa, who saw them and crouched down stealthily. From under the sink she grabbed a small stick. She stood up and aimed carefully. She wound up, smacked and killed them. The kids lifted their eyes momentarily, as if the blow had disturbed them. Then a raucous, strident sound was heard, like old eggs exploding in a fire, but without any eggs and without any fire, and Rosa pulled out her little mirror and squealed happily. The raucous sound stopped. Inside the little mirror there was an elf, and Rosa turned it around to position it in front of the kids. The elf looked like Rosa, with thin, drawn-on eyebrows and painted lids. But tiny, and wearing a headband and a pink bathrobe. Her house was small. Elfin. The whole thing fit inside there. The kids said hello to the elf, the bell on the urn rang, and Rosa grabbed the mug and left the kitchen to go back upstairs.

When Margarida heard her prattering on and coming up the stairs, she snorted and rolled her eyes. And when Rosa entered the bedroom with Bernadeta's chamomile tea, Margarida turned her chair, indignant, because she just could not understand why that annoying outsider didn't have a home of her own, and always had to be coming into other people's houses. Why she didn't have her own mother or grandmother or sister. Or aunties. She had to have a mother. Everyone has a mother, whether they want one or not. Or a sister. Heck. Anything! Rosa stroked the old woman's hands and showed her the elf inside her little mirror, even though Bernadeta couldn't care less. Rosa's fingernails were inordinately long and purple, and it alarmed Margarida to see that Bernadeta let herself be touched by those claws. And not only did she let herself be touched, she even seemed to be enjoying it. But then she thought how no one had ever loved Bernadeta. That Àngela hadn't cuddled with her when she was a little girl. And that must be why she liked that horrid cooing and stroking. When Rosa looked at Bernadeta, all she saw was a helpless little old lady lying in a bed, but there is no such thing as a helpless little old lady. Just wait and see, you innocents! Wait until Bernadeta dies. And see where she goes. That fiendish woman, the lost lamb who brought the roaring lion into the house, slipped him in like the plague, infections and curses, with his retinue, she'd welcomed him with palm leaves and laurel branches. Because Margarida didn't have a shadow of a doubt as to where the old lady was headed when she died. Or that they'd have to tie her down. She'd follow that stench like a trail. Filthy, sinful, and slippery as she was. She would insert herself into the night like a bitch walking on two legs, with socks and a nightgown, and she would look for the devil among the trees!

Rosa went out into the parlor and sat at the table. She asked the elf how's work going and the elf said good, and asked questions. Rosa responded and said names, she said Bernadeta and David, she said Marta, Sheila, and Nico. And suddenly she laughed, because the elf inside the little mirror was carrying on. Rosa covered her mouth with her hands, her fingers on her cheeks. And in the midst of the uproar, Sheila and Nico went up the stairs and interrupted their mother, saying they were hungry. When are we leaving, Mom? they asked. And when Margarida heard those voices in the darkness coming up the stairs, searching for their mother, she shivered. Rosa told them that they'd leave when Marta came back. That she was talking to Auntie Carme. That their supper was all ready, in a Tupperware container in the bag, and they could heat it up in the microwave. Whatever those words meant.

Margarida called her children *my sons*, but Bartomeu and Esteve no longer came searching for her, they no longer asked for her, and they no longer called her *Mama*. They looked at her with disdain, because while Margarida was locked up in the Veguer prison, they had grown big and surly, like cats who grow up and forget who their mother is. And when they left, never to return, by night as if escaping, they didn't even say goodbye to her. And then Margarida understood. With her heart like a pine nut. Her sons' bed was empty and the blankets were cold, and Margarida understood. She knew that because of the pact that Joana had made and broken with the devil, she was missing a quarter of her heart and Blanca was missing a tongue. That all-yellow sister of hers named Esperança had been born without a liver. The heir had been missing an asshole. Esteve, an ear; Guilla, a name; Àngela, the ability to feel pain; Martí the Lame, a small stretch of leg; and Bernadeta, eyelashes. Later on she would understand that Dolça was missing her goat tail, Marta had no memory, and Alexandra, goodness knows what Alexandra was missing! Everything! Patience, a spirit of sacrifice, blood in her veins, motivation, respect . . . But when her sons left, Margarida grasped what it was that Bartomeu was missing, what her first-born had always been missing, the missing thing she'd searched and searched for when he was an infant and that she couldn't find, because it was hidden: it was the love a son should feel for his mother.

From that moment on, all Margarida did was wait to die. But alas!, everyone cut ahead of that poor, luckless woman. As if it were a race. Everyone in a throng. Elisabet was first. She died pissing blood and sticking out her tongue and jeering with her hands. Later, the Martís and Guilla, who should never have left the farmhouse. Ever since they were little, Margarida had said that to them again and again, and yet they went and got themselves killed so far from the house that they didn't know how to get back once they were dead. Then Àngela, like a piece of cured ham, dried out and parched on the inside because she didn't know how to cry. At that point, Margarida realized that the farmhouse was hers again, hers and Joana's and Blanca's. With no outsiders. Like before. She didn't even count Bernadeta, because that fiend who remembered what wasn't hers to remember lived hidden like a spider. And for a moment Margarida celebrated that the house was hers again, for her and Joana and Blanca. And it could've been lovely, all three of them living together again, as a mother and two sisters, if Joana and Blanca had been happy about it. But they weren't happy about it. And not only were they not happy about it, but they'd said, every woman for herself, fare thee well! Blanca choked on a turnip. Her head fell into her soup, and Margarida had to pull her face out of the plate. Joana died laughing. Her head, filled with nonsense, fables, and jokes, hung to one side. Margarida found her sitting on the bench with her neck bent, her mouth agape, and her eyes smiling. And poor Margarida was left all alone, and she would kneel in the evenings, supplicant. She would close her eyes and she'd see the gates of heaven opening to receive her. The angels, oh, how they sang. With their plump pink lips, their velvety cheeks, their eyes damp with joy, their gold crowns, and their silk tunics, barefoot and playing lutes. And amid the angels was Our Lord, who took her face in His hands and kissed her. *Welcome to my Eternal Glory*, He would murmur to her. Just as He'd said to Francesc when He welcomed him. When He took him from that dreadful square and sheltered him in His paternal arms. *Welcome to my Eternal Glory*, He had whispered in his ear, and He had taken hold of his sturdy, rough hands to cover them in kisses. Because Our Lord had kissed Francesc's thick fingers, his palms, the backs of his hands, his wrists. Then He had looked at him, and He had kissed his forehead, two kisses on his clean cheeks, more kisses between his eyebrows, on his nose, on his Adam's apple, on the cleft in his chin, on his lips. The mouths of the Lord and of Francesc had opened up moist and luscious, and they had come together. Their tongues had collided, like in a battle, making twisty somersaults, their hands seeking, touching, groping. Heavy moans of pleasure suddenly roused Margarida from her sleep. Flushed. Agitated. Sweaty. Seething in turmoil. It was pitch black. But the sounds from her dream continued. The banging and the grunting. At first she thought it was mice. But amid the heavy breathing, Margarida could make out whispers. And she sat up, convinced someone had snuck into the house. Thieves! Evildoers! After being hidden for centuries, they'd found them. The walls breathed, damp, rhythmic, mournful, halfway between grousing and something else. Ravenous, like a mouth. The laments grew louder, then muffled. They turned into shrieks. And Margarida's heart, small, throbbing, compact, scared but at the same time curious, pushed open a door like an eyelid. And then, God save us all, she saw it. The terrible vision. The vile embrace. Perfidious. The naked buttocks. The white skin and the black hair. Bernadeta. And the sinister stain behind Bernadeta, with its thick neck and hunched back. The bull. The tail, the horns. The devil inside the house! The open mouths. The sweat turned into pearls. The pudendum and the breasts. The panting. The moaning. The thrusts. One after the other, one after the other. All that fit within Margarida's eyes was the bull and the woman and the buttocks and the bellies. And inside her nose all that fit was the abhorrent stench of sex, of goat, of feet, of ass, of stagnant water, of nether regions. Margarida was breathing heavily. So many centuries of hiding, so many years of cloaking!, the decaying bones of a life that counted for a dozen human lives!, so lonely, burdened, and long, devoted to watching over that farmhouse, and all of it, for what? For that god-killer to come and let the devil himself into the house. Margarida tried to return to her room, tried to lean on the shifting walls. But she'd fallen to her knees. She was trembling. Her hands were interlaced. The fingernails were first pink, then white. The time had come. They had killed her. What she'd seen was so ugly that it had killed her. And she still had time to think, hallelujah! But not to apprehend that when someone has a bad death, a ghastly death, an execrable death so horrific that God can't bear to watch, then that someone is left behind and wanders through this world doomed. Like a lost soul. Forsaken. Neglected, abandoned, cursed, and castigated. Fare thee well! she gasped, surrendered and beaten. Eager and inflamed. Desirous of reaching the other side. Expecting the circle of angels.

NIGHT

Ahir es va morir la besàvia
l'àvia també s'ha de morir
la mort de la mare es prepara
i tu, more't pels teus fills!
PAU RIBA, "JA S'HA MORT LA BESÀVIA"*

The pong was organic. Alive. Scratchy. Dense. Prickly. It throbbed and oozed, tenacious, swollen with the dark and the damp. The women in the kitchen were restless. Keyed up. They stirred nervously and banged impatiently on whatever was at hand. It infected the children. As they ate dinner they tapped their feet rhythmically against the legs of the table. Rosa was also uneasy. She paced upstairs, and then they heard her come down, open the built-in cabinet in the entryway, pull out a jar, and shake it. She held it out in front of her, arm extended, and from the jar came a concentrated and strong-smelling air that went ffsst, ffsst.

---

* Great-Grandma died yesterday / Grandma will have to die too / Mother is next in line / and then you, die for your kids!

She scattered it all over the entryway. She went back upstairs and squirted the floral wind in the parlor. Then came the sound of a horseless carriage, and Sheila exclaimed, finally! The girl leaped up and put her hands on her hips. When the front door opened, she said, there's no baby goat! Marta wiped her shoes before coming in. She shrugged. She replied that it had certainly been there that morning. And that goats can escape through a hole this big. She brought two fingers together. She took off her wet jacket and added that if she found the kid tomorrow, she'd give it to her. That she'd had enough, of goats and kids, that Bernadeta was old and didn't take care of them anymore. But Rosa, who heard her as she was coming down the stairs, complained that a goat was the last thing she needed! Does it smell bad in here to you, Marta? she asked. Sheila said, it sure does. Rosa added that she'd sprayed air freshener, but that she wasn't sure it had helped much. Then she commented that Bernadeta was already sleeping, and that she hadn't wanted dinner, just cookies, and Marta said, thank you, Rosa.

But Bernadeta was not asleep in the bedroom upstairs. She was only pretending. She had woken up in the afternoon, when Rosa and her children had arrived, and she hadn't been able to get back to sleep. She had closed her eyes for long stretches so that sleep would come looking for her, but there was no way for her to climb back into that deep well. She heard the distant and muffled voices of Rosa and Marta in the entryway. They were laughing. Rosa was saying, my goodness, this house goes on and on, Marta! And she assured her that she wouldn't know what to do with that ginormous farmhouse, with all its nooks, and all its noises, and all its silences, and she added that today, with the clatter of the rain, she could almost hear whispering and laughing, banging and walking around. Marta laughed, and Sheila asked, ghosts, Mom? If she could avoid it, Bernadeta didn't deal with anyone who wasn't Marta, Alexandra, the doctor who visited her at the farmhouse, since she refused to leave, and Rosa and her kids. Marta and Alexandra were her granddaughter and great-granddaughter. The doctor was aloof. And Rosa was affable and, in fact, almost never brought her children with her to work at Mas Clavell, keeping Bernadeta company while Marta was at the factory. There was the sound of jingling keys and Rosa shouting, let's get a move on! so Sheila and Nico would get into their coats. Say goodbye, she ordered, and the kids said goodbye and left the house. Bernadeta was prepared. She could feel her body exhausted, her heart tranquil, her spirit frail. Her eyes were closed, her jaw slack, her tongue soft inside her mouth. She breathed in, adjusted her head on the pillow, pursed her lips, and put her hands on her chest. She had to fall asleep. She sighed. She had envisioned it since she was a little girl, that she would die sleeping in her bed. Sometimes it seemed within reach. That she was already there. That a sweet listlessness was swaddling her, that her lips were disengaging, her bones sinking into her flesh, and that she was already dreaming, already dreaming. But then all sorts of hands would grip her and hold her head up in the air. Bernadeta was a little girl and she struggled but couldn't free herself. The sky was piercing. She wanted to close her eyelids, but she couldn't, because fingers were holding them open. She tried to wriggle free, but they pinned her down even tighter, and they poured tepid golden water into her sore eyes, a shock that blurred their faces. Only then would they let her go. And Bernadeta blinked. She figured that something had changed, and she realized that they no longer stung. That the pang of remorse had abated. Her cheeks were damp. Her eyes were fresh, soothed, like two pools after a storm. Until they dried out. And the stinging returned. More rabid. More irate. The fingers pushed her eyelids open, and again

Bernadeta cried copper tears until the pain lessened. She remained still. Static. With her eyes wide. Sometimes opening and closing them, because they no longer hurt. But then, when the hands left her alone, she would see them. First there was a man with black orifices on either side of his head where his ears should've been, moaning because they were ripping the flesh from his loins with pincers. Bernadeta shut her lids, but the man was still there. She whimpered, and they poured more thyme water into her eyes as if they were drowning them. Then she spied a swollen purple baby with no hole back there. The infant howled and howled, and Bernadeta looked at him in terror until he was no longer howling, because he was dead and being buried. The hands squeezed her tighter. The more she whimpered, the more infusions they poured into her. And the stinging didn't return, but the more bucketfuls of thyme-infused water they gave her, the more gullies and channels, crevices and chasms opened up behind her eyes, and the more things she saw. Wolves, everywhere. Wolves eating children. Wolves vomiting with foamy mouths and their tails between their legs. She could make out a man with the face of a dog and straw hair, hanged on a gallows up on a mountain. And then more hanged men in all sorts of squares, and more quartered men. She watched as three people entered a farmhouse and stabbed the owners, their daughter, the servant, and the maid. Her mother would shout, *You're making it up!* and *Shut up!* But the girl did not shut up, because then she would see a pile of dirty, naked bodies, like worms, beneath the trees, with open mouths and white cheeks. And in that pile of disjointed faces, there was the face of her uncle, and the face of her father. If she studied the pile more carefully, she also found the face of her brother. And Bernadeta would cry, but she cried tears of rage, not of sorrow. Because everyone loved Martí the Lame and everyone turned their backs on her. Her father would cry out, *Who could possibly kill me, when we are hidden here?!*, but if Bernadeta touched him, Martí the Tenderhearted would pull his hands away.

Until the day she saw the bull. The only comely thing that Bernadeta had ever laid eyes upon. Majestic. Tranquil and bovine. As lovely as the loveliest thing. Protective and black. Then she caught a glimpse of the kitten. A calico cat. Sweet. Fluffy. With a pink tongue. Later she saw the small goat, and Bernadeta stopped crying, because she liked the goat. Clever. Good. Serene. Sometimes it was a white nanny goat, sometimes it was a black billy. And it would keep Bernadeta company, so she wouldn't see the yellow baby or the woman whose face and hands had been devoured by beasts. And as she grew, she learned. To seek out the bull. To console herself with the kitten. And when she saw Blanca's face fall into her soup, or how those soldiers set the house aflame, or how Joana suffered an apoplexy with her eyes rolled back into her head and her tongue out, Bernadeta, who was already a young lady, would frantically search for the bald man with magnificent eyebrows, the toes of a rooster, and the breasts of a woman. When Margarida barked, *Get lost!* and *Don't look at me! If not even my death is mine and only mine, what is!*, Bernadeta would obey her, and look away, and instead of watching Margarida, with her eyes like two buttercup squashes, dead on the ground, she would seek out the goat. And when even as a full-grown woman she was pursued by those evildoers who stabbed everyone in the house, and the hanged men and the quartered ones, she would look for the bull. And she wouldn't see how they were knifed, nor how they were chopped into pieces, nor the child swollen with excrement, nor the man with the turds and the vipers, nor the blue vomiting wolves, because the bull was as big as an embrace, and nothing more fit into her eyes. Even when her mother demanded to know

Where are they? and *What do you know?*, Bernadeta took comfort in looking at the bull, the cat, the billy goat and the nanny, and the man whose mouth was ugly and pretty at the same time. At first she kept quiet, because she knew what would happen to her mother if she answered. But Àngela had been so insistent, *I want you to tell me* and *What else? What else? What else?!*, that Bernadeta had explained to her how they'd killed her father, her uncle, and her brother, and then Àngela had died of grief, withered like a hunk of salt pork.

The old woman closed her eyes obstinately and sought out a stretch of bed that was still cool. She pulled the covers up to her chin. She listened to the cradling sound of the rain, and she breathed deeply. But the smell wasn't helping. The thick scent filling the house was too good, too exciting, too intoxicating and stimulating, too filled with promises. It slunk into her nose, and she was run through with an intense warmth and shivers that at her advanced age seemed unthinkable.

Bernadeta had always been so alone that the first time she smelled the pong she didn't believe it. The thick stench of beast, of bull, of goat, and of even more things that came out of the forest and clambered along the ground. Bernadeta knelt down like someone praying. She inhaled. And she followed the waft like a trail. On all fours. Thrilled, with her nostrils throbbing and her knees trembling, because she had an inkling of whom that scent belonged to. She found a vein of pure, stifling putridness. So pungent it was blinding. She trailed it, leading with her hands, feeling her way. In fits and starts. Like a blind woman. First she hit upon a rock wall. Which was damp and cold. Then she found the hole with her fingers. Which was low, three hand spans by four. A spring of pestilence. She lay face down and wriggled inside, like a snake, or a slug, or something being reborn. She squirmed with her belly, with her thighs, with her elbows. Pursuing that wet and virulent stench. The mouth of the den was narrow and then it grew wide and oval like an almond. Bernadeta extended her neck to get her nose in. She extended her hands to get her fingers in. She felt the ground and the walls, and in the midst of the blackness she found a hoof. Like a jolt. Hard, cloven. And another hoof. Also hard and cloven. Her fingers were humming. She touched a hairy belly. Her hands burned. She groped a chest covered in rough fur, a puny skull, a curved neck, low ears, short horns, closed eyes. The snout, rounded, stank of piss and ash. The animal was sleeping. Bernadeta said, *Where were you? Where were you?* Her voice came out shouting, *WHERE WERE YOU?! WHERE WERE YOU?!*, and the devil woke up on her lap, in the dark, startled, awkward, rebuked. They didn't see each other. The he-goat—because then it was a he-goat, ugly, begging, withered, grotesque, horned, and hunchbacked from the weight of so much solitude—opened his snout, at first surprised, then tantalized. Bernadeta brought her mouth close to his. The tongue of the beast was salty, spicy with anise, and earthy. The woman felt his hairy skin and the flesh beneath. And the caresses made the he-goat grow. His chest swelled, his back filled out, and his neck became thick like a tree. Bernadeta touched his horns, which were now long and curved, his ears were fleshy, his forehead wide, his snout wet, his neck veiny. No longer a he-goat. Now it was a bull. Black. Immense and lush. Bernadeta, hungry, couldn't get enough. She pecked at his hard flesh, his abundant curves, his sturdiness and protuberances, until the bull slipped into her embrace, shrinking in her arms and becoming first a small purring cat, and then an unusually long, skinny man with the toes of a rooster, the breasts of a woman, and responsive hands.

Bernadeta began to slither into that den every day, and within the dark belly of the mountain, she would cling to that unstable, changing body. She would open her eyes, and the only thing she would see was blue darkness. Violet, black, purple. Dancing, until suddenly the shadows would burst. Gleaming, orange, yellow, scarlet. For a moment light would rip through the blackness. Then the obscurity would swallow it up. First the bright flashes, then the dark. And more brilliance, and even more shadows. But in that murkiness there were no earless men, no faceless women, no babies bloated with excrement, no yellow newborns, no vipers, no wolves, no hanged nor quartered men, no violated women, no stab victims. Only fires. Only a never-ending night sky. And sudden blasts. Brilliance. And stars. And then an endless storm. It rained and rained, and it rained so much that the unremitting rain made the seas and rivers and lakes. The water was black and moved forward. Then it retreated. And the sea opened up and fire came out of the wound. Like blood. The clouds grew wispy and you could make out a sun, like a flower. New. First white. Later murderous yellow. It began to hum as soon as it rose. The moon was fat and pink, as if you could touch it. The stars flamed and collapsed, blue with streaking tails. There were no houses, no trees, no mountains. There was no farmhouse called Mas Clavell, because everything was covered in water. The stars bolted into it. Billows of smoke came out of it. And the water churned, ripped, and the mountain ranges clawed at the sky, deafening, as they rose. But the stars never stopped falling. And the clouds returned and brought the cold, and with the cold, the ice. The sea froze over, white. It thawed, blue. And then came the heat, which dried up everything. Then the ice returned. And again the heat. And later the moss and the shrubs and the trees that emerged from the water, and the insects that flew, and the flowers, and the fish that walked. But the cold never flagged, nor did the heat, nor the clouds, nor the darkness, nor the ugly frogs, nor the sour-faced toads, nor the armadillo bugs, which were as big as goats, nor the centipedes like snakes, nor the lizards like horses, nor the monstrous hens with teeth instead of beaks, and hairy hides and scaly hides and feathered hides, which killed one another and ate one another.

There came a knock at the door. Tock, tock. Marta, who was downstairs, said, coming. She opened up. On the other side was Sheila, with her jacket over her head to protect herself from the rain. She said that she had forgotten her backpack, and Bernadeta could hear through the stairwell how Marta's voice exclaimed, you're as bad as me, so absentminded! The girl's trotting entered the kitchen and exited it. Sheila said a fleeting bye, and Marta closed the door, but Bernadeta, up in the bedroom, thought that since Margarida's death, the world had shrunk, and it had become difficult, impossible, for her to hide. And now someone was always knocking on that door. One after the other.

Tock, tock, they knocked. Bernadeta opened up. There were three men. Three young men. It was raining and the air was damp and smelled of wet leaves. They said, *Good evening, ma'am*, and they looked in fear at the woman holding the door open, with her lashless yellow lizard eyes. Bernadeta watched. One of them explained, *We scarcely made it out, ma'am!* Bernadeta did not respond. They had pale faces, dark circles under their eyes, sunken cheeks. They wore soaked espadrilles, their clothing clung to their bones. *We scarcely made it out with our lives.* They introduced themselves. The water splattered them. The one who spoke went by the name of Pernales; his cousin was Vampiro. They had dark eyes and hair. The third one, who was bowing his head and getting the wettest, and who was blond and pink-skinned, was called Cachorro. "Puppy." As if they were playing. Pernales spoke in his splendid and convincing voice: *Like dead men walking!* he uttered. *We had a cave that seemed like a good spot, and we thought it was sturdy and that there was no need to brace it.* Vampiro, the cousin, whose tone was sour, tired, and sad, put in his two cents: *I said it needed bracing.* But Pernales continued, *We didn't brace anything, because there were big stones on top. And it seemed like a good cave. Well hidden, narrow at first and then wide, like an almond.* Bernadeta groaned, but with the din from the storm, they didn't hear her groan, and Pernales added, *And it was raining this afternoon, and we said,* Let's go out! With this rain no one will be out, and we can walk a little in the daylight; *we'd almost forgotten how. And we hadn't gone more than a hundred meters when I said to this guy,* You got the skin? *The wineskin. And we didn't have it. And we went back for it. But when we got there the cave had collapsed. We had hardly been out much more than a moment! Had we dawdled any longer, we'd've been buried alive!* And then Pernales said, as if someone had asked, *Our levy was taken to Barcelona by a civil servant. And out of thirty-five of us or more, only a dozen went, because everyone else was either in hiding or volunteering on the front. After the physical and the enlistment, they let us go back home, but when we left the blockhouse it was one in the morning and the inns were closed. And we had to sleep out in the open, in the Plaça Catalunya, until it was time for the first train.* Bernadeta wasn't listening to him, but Pernales said that it was on that night, sleeping outside, that he first started to think about not going to the war, about maybe hiding in the forest. *Because my parents would be upset whether I went to the front or joined the Nationalists. And then my cousin*—and he pointed to the sad man beside him—*told me that he wasn't going to fight, that he was going into hiding.* And Cousin Vampiro added, taciturnly, *Rather than the front . . . a slaughterhouse . . .* Pernales explained, *First we hid in the forest near home, so we could still help out. Until one day they almost caught us. We'd* come down from our patch of forest to have breakfast and find some grub, and we were sitting around the table when my little brother sticks his head out of the window and shouts, The carabineers are coming! And there was no time, so instead of going down the stairs we jumped out the window. Luckily, my sister spotted my jacket hanging in the entryway, and she stuffed it into the pot where they boil cabbage for the pigs. They searched everywhere, top to bottom, but they didn't think to look inside that pot. And they kept asking, Where is your brother and your cousin, and they said they didn't know, that we'd gone off to war and they hadn't seen us since. And they asked the children, Where's your brother? Where's your cousin? and the children responded, Gone to kill fascists!, and when they threatened to take away my mother, she told them, Go ahead and take me if you want. Just let me grab my knitting, so I can make some socks . . . Don't know where those young men went off to . . . Bernadeta saw them, without wanting to see them, hidden in the forest, as Pernales said, And then we didn't go near that house again, and instead, every three or four days, my father would bring us things we couldn't get ourselves, out there in our hidey-hole, and he would give us news of the war. Until they took him, poor Dad. Because his son and his nephew were absent from duty, and they knew it. And then it was Uncle Carlos who'd come and bring us grub. Bernadeta glimpsed a scrawny man who brought them food, but she didn't know whether it was the father or Uncle Carlos. Nor did she care. Uncle Carlos would tell us about the prisoners. Because they arrested men and women from all the houses that had relatives in hiding. Forty men and forty women, wives and mothers of the deserters. And at first they said that if they paid a hundred and fifty duros for every man in hiding, they'd let them go, but then they said no, that if the sons or husbands or whoever they were didn't show up for duty, their relatives would stay in jail. But my sister went to see our father, and *he said that no way did he want us to give ourselves up.* The cousin, Vampiro, added, *If it weren't for the prisoners, I wouldn't care how long the war lasted—another year, or two.* The blond young man fell silent. Pernales jabbered on, *Then we went deeper into the forest because things were getting thorny. Didn't want to cause trouble for those at home. And we kept still, very still, in the forest, and only at night would we do our gymnastics or commandeer some fava beans or potatoes. But, ma'am, we were very careful about who we commandeered them from. And if we were starting to think that people might be on to us, we looked for a different spot in the forest. And then we found this guy all by his lonesome and we took him with us, because just look at that puppy face . . .* , he said, and pointed to the little blond guy. *Before the war he was headed to the seminary, and he knows everything there is to know about drawing!* And there in the rain he exclaimed, *Show her, Cachorro, show her how good you draw.* And the young man who had been headed to the seminary before the war pulled a sheaf of yellow pages from underneath his shirt. *We didn't know that there was a house so close by*, he murmured, and that was all he said. But Pernales continued, as if it were dangerous to remain silent and have to wait for this distressing woman to respond, *And then we found that cave shaped like an almond, and now this guy teaches us how to draw, and we just keep watch and draw all day.* The drawings, which were of donkeys, pigs, horses, a dog, and a girl with a branch, were getting wet. And then Pernales complained, *It was such a good hideout, that little cave we'd found, because it was low, three by four handspans, a badger's cave; you had to crawl to get in. First your head. And what shitty luck that today, with all this rain, it's caved in!* Bernadeta shut the door. And bolted it. The young men banged on it, and shouted, *Please, ma'am, we aren't armed, we're very hungry, the little we had got buried, give us something to eat.* But Bernadeta wouldn't have given them anything even if she'd had something to give. *Please, ma'am, if they find us they'll kill us.* Let them find you, let them kill you, she thought.

Bernadeta stroked his cat whiskers, his belly with eight nipples and womanly breasts, his hooves, his horns, his veiny neck, his goat's udder. She called him by every name. She whispered them into his ear. All at the same time. She called him Pretty Thing and Ugly Thing, Barn Owl and Hellion, Stranger and Nasty Part. She called him Slayer and Thief of Life, Beloved and Fallen Star, Beast, Shadow King, Rogue, Dragon and Prince of Darkness, Serpent of Old, He-Goat, Tailless Imp, Goatskin and Tempter; she called him Crow, Old Hornie, Baphomet, Little Horns, and Greenhorn. She heard him laughing in the darkness. His was a guttural laugh, and Bernadeta gulped it down because it reeked of damp rock, of anise, and of semen. She would whisper to him, Old Harry, and Lucifer, Gleam in My Eyes and the Sun and the Stars, Midday Sun, Angel of the Bottomless Pit, Kitty, First Sinner, Adversary, Cacodemon, Cloven-Hoofed, Deceiver, Bugbear, Devilkins, Bringer of the Dawn, Son of Perdition, Long-Tailed and Short-Tailed, Xiribelles, Lord of the Night, Angel of Light, Scapegrace, Long-Tailed Fart, Beginning and End, Rapscallion, and Scallywag.

But sometimes the demon slipped through her arms. And he didn't turn into a docile kitten, or a haughty bull, or a kind goat, but a miserable lump. Afflicted detritus, a sad and solitary hulk that didn't want to be loved or to love. An ugly and pathetic man, a malnourished nanny goat with head bowed, a melancholy and remorseful bull that wanted only to sleep, curled up and covered by a heavy cape of grief, embroidered with pearls. A decrepit he-goat, buried under an entire mountain of remote recollections that didn't include Bernadeta. He moaned and was wistful for times gone by. For other companions. The huge bonfires and the bastard beasts. The flutes. The splatters of limpid water from pools and lagoons. The scent of crumpled grass. Laughter like bells. The enterprises of old. Erstwhile works and tasks. From before, when he was a giant. When he was an always-joyful goat. Wild. Savage. Firstborn. Neither just nor unjust, neither good nor bad. When he was a monster with fiery eyes, a winged beast with hooves and horns. With human arms and goat legs. He reminisced about times past when he'd had an entourage, and they would encircle him, offering him fruit and cheeses, and they would comb and adorn his hair and beard with flowers. Before, when they wanted him, when they needed him, when they called for him, when they made sacrifices to him and asked for him, on their knees, nude, smeared with unguents, dancing with their asses on display. He recounted the souls. The ones he'd garnered and the ones he'd lost, like a jackass. The soul of that old guy from Sant Hilari, who'd wanted to cross the gully one morning when the torrent was full. The soul of that lass from Girona, who had to get married on the other side of the Ter, and on her wedding day the river was high. The soul of the lady of Can Besa, who wanted a well. The soul of that ugly woman from Seva, who wanted a husband with an inheritance. The soul of the lord of Montclús, who begged for his riches to be returned to him. The soul of the heir to the house called Molí Nou, who coveted the love of a girl who was entirely indifferent to him. The soul of the Quintanes heir, who asked for the same thing but from a different damsel. The souls of the provosts of Sant Antoni, who couldn't find an orchestra. The soul of Queló from Gurb, who never finished his reaping in time. The soul of that noble from Castell de les Escaules, who wanted a smooth road. And the soul of that carter from Els Hostalets, who loaded up his cart too high, and his mules couldn't make it down the slope. Bernadeta murmured sweet nothings to him, but he turned his back. *I am he whom no one loves*, he would say to her. And Bernadeta should have guessed it. She should have seen it coming, she who sees everything: that a capricious and volatile creature always leaves. Always flees. Always hides. Always slips away, craven. Like a fawn, like a snake, like a rat. But she didn't want to see it. Because all she wanted, please, pretty please, was for her friend to play with her again and embrace her and look at her with little goat eyes. And then she discovered that the farmhouse healed him. That the house cured his melancholy and grief. They had never let him come inside. They made him stay in the garden, on the threshing floor. Like an animal. And if she said to him, *Let's go to the farmhouse*, the mewling kitten's eyes gleamed. The nanny goat pricked up her ears. The bull revived. The man with rooster toes forgot about his moaning and self-pitying. They would enter by night. The demon made a serious face as he walked through the door. Excited. Naughty. He looked at the dark entryway, with his head held high and his mouth slightly open. He took in the beams, the doors, the windows. He touched the walls. He went into the kitchen, absorbed, and looked at the fireplace. The table, the chairs. The ceiling. They went upstairs. He caressed the steps. He circled through the parlor. He bent his knees and lifted his rooster toes. First one, then the other. He raised his shoulders up to his ears and stretched his arms into the air. He danced. He opened his eyes, like two wells, and smiled with his ugly mouth. Beautiful. Voluptuous. Joyful. With his hunched back, he drew close to Bernadeta. They embraced, and they rubbed up against each other. They thrust against the darkness, against the steps. And Bernadeta bit him, like an apple, like a fig, like a pomegranate. She swallowed, and refused to release her bite, even though she no longer had her teeth clamped onto a man's shoulder but onto the nape of a sweet kitten or onto the neck of a fierce bull who barely fit inside the parlor.

But they were still knocking. Tock, tock. Like madmen. TOCK, TOCK. They shouted, *Open up! OPEN UP! OPEN UP!* They threatened to bust down the door if she didn't open it. And Bernadeta thought, Go ahead, bust it down. Bust it down. Because she couldn't care less. But they didn't bust it down. A slender man with a jacket and a rifle came into the house through the kitchen window. He opened the bolt on the big door and three more men came in. They weren't those boys called Pernales, Vampiro, and Cachorro. They were armed and they weren't soaked, because it was no longer raining. And it was no longer night, but day. The light filtering through the door was velvety and pink. They pounced on Bernadeta. One of the men, with blue eyes and a red face, grabbed her by the hair. The one who'd come in through the window pointed to her and said, *She's with child. Look at her belly.* Bernadeta looked at her belly. They let go of her hair and they lifted her, one man at each arm. A third man, who wore a beret and had a mustache, asked, *Where are you hiding them?* Then the third, who was short and squat, spat and exclaimed, *This house stinks like an animal den.* And he lectured her: *The comrades in the various anti-fascist sectors fight and die on the battlefields in service to the cause that benefits us all. And when the bad sons of the people hide and flee like cowards, forgetting their duties in the war against fascism, they sit at the traitors' banquet table.* Bernadeta could scarcely see or hear him. The man added that those three turncoats who were named Josep and Pere Casas and Frederic Amorós, even though they'd introduced themselves to her as Pernales, Vampiro, and Cachorro, respectively, had confessed when they'd captured them—confessed that it was she who had helped them. Brought them food and blankets. And they'd declared that her house was chockablock with deserters. With cowards hiding like rats. They turned the entire house over. The one with the lovely blue eyes in the middle of his hardened, red-face—he watched over her. Saying, *Where is he? Where have you hidden him, the one who gave you that belly?*

Bernadeta hadn't seen these men coming, because, in her embrace with the devil, she had seen only the sky falling. In chunks. The cold returning. The snow and the ice. The famished beasts. Then more eruptions, ripping, and sparks. Smoke billowing orange, lilac, red. The rain of fire. And the black clouds. The hens like cows and the feathered lizards lay in the shadows, mouths open. The trees slept beneath the snow. The rivers, beneath the ash. The night was identical to the day. The day identical to the night. And then a sun appeared with a white blouse, distant and sickly, and carried off the mist. But the dry, cracked trees, fallen, burned, and ripped out by the roots, had seen it. And very carefully and very deliberately, they stretched out skinny sprouts of green leaves like fingers seeking out that sun. And very cautiously, slowly, the whiskers of the survivors appeared, the tiny clawed feet, the ears, the teeth. The small beasties that had hidden themselves away. Mice, weasels, squirrels, dormice, rats, shrews, moles. When Bernadeta found Margarida dead on the ground with her hands clasped, her eyes and mouth open, she didn't think she'd been left alone in the house, because she'd always been alone. And she didn't see it, the terrible solitude like a slap across the face, until the stench left. Suddenly. Just as it had come. Sneaking off. On tiptoe. And one morning you could no longer smell it anywhere. Bernadeta shouted, because she saw herself splayed out. Legs open. In the kitchen. Split in half. With her belly swollen and immense, all alone, giving birth to a baby girl. And she looked for him. She closed her eyes and searched for the devil in every single day and every night that lay before her, until she died, as she'd told her brother she would die, in her bed, old, dreaming. But she never found the demon. He had left. She ran, stumbling, to the rock wall, and she said, *Where are you going? Why are you leaving?* She screamed the words, *WHERE ARE YOU GOING?! WHY ARE YOU LEAVING?!* Then she howled like a madwoman, *I SAW IT!* She screamed, *COWARD!* She shrieked, *I SAW YOU LEAVING!* No one responded. Bernadeta moaned, *Coward, coward, coward!* She crawled into the cave, shrieking like a vixen, bellowing, *WHY ARE YOU LEAVING? WHY ARE YOU LEAVING?* She clawed at the cold inside the den, the blackness, the dampness, the ground. Still there was no response. And then she roared, *IF YOU'RE LEAVING, THEN GO!* She saw nothing. *GET GONE. Go and don't come back.* She insulted him, *Traitor, liar, thief, trickster, devious abandoner, miserable blasphemer, coward.* She was crying. But he did not respond. She imagined him curled up in the shadows, head down, pitiful, incapable. *Coward, coward, coward!* Then she thought with horror that perhaps he wasn't even in there. She scratched at the air. She pounded the walls, she threw herself against them, and with each pointless lunge she repeated, *Begone. Go, but don't ever come back!,* and with as much cruelty as she could muster, *If you go, don't ever come back. If you go, don't come back. Don't come back until I'm dead, because if you come back before that, I won't want to see you and I won't want to love you. Don't come back until the day I die.* She left the hole and covered it with rocks heavier than herself.

Where are you hiding him?! shouted the man with the ruddy face and the blue eyes. He pointed to her belly. Bernadeta quickly returned. To the rocky den. Remorseful. Cooled off. Sorry. She removed the rocks covering the hole, her nails covered in blood. She went inside again, crawling, crying, asking for forgiveness.

Where is he?! The man was forcing her chin up, but Bernadeta couldn't see him. He wasn't there. No one was there inside. There below. Only that watery and painful trail, increasingly invaded by the scent of wet rock and box plants outside. Bernadeta coiled up, sick, desolate, torn. She hugged her knees, and the sobs came in fits and starts, but there was no consoling her. *Who gave you this belly?!* The man shook her chin. And then Bernadeta came face to face with those blue eyes, and she said, cold as frost, *The devil.* Then she laughed like a madwoman. The others had searched the house and come up empty. They encircled her like hunting dogs. Bernadeta grabbed her belly loaded with poison and began to speak, tranquil, serious. Cruel. She looked first at the one with blue eyes. She told him, *The slide on your pistol will break.* The man wore his hair combed straight back. His eyes were so pretty. *You will shoot at the backs of men fleeing, and the slide of your pistol will plunge deep into one of your own eyes. You will miss the men completely, and your eye will ooze like the yolk of an egg.* She smiled. *You will scream. But you will not die right away. No. You will die slowly, from an infection.* She turned. She pointed at the one with the mustache and the beret. She yelled at him, *You!* He was frightened. She liked that he was frightened. He should be frightened. *They will sing with wide mouths and raised fists. As they kill you. They will have you all penned in like hens, with barbed wire, on a foreign beach. All sand and wind and sea and black-skinned soldiers to whom you can't make yourself understood. You will go to the latrine alone, and your comrades will kill you. With your pants down at your ankles. Two will hold you and one will stab you, and they will sing.* She searched for another one. *You!* She was looking at the shortest one, the one who had lectured her, and she laughed. *You, they'll hang.* She laughed harder because of the man's expression. *They will find you at your house, because you will not flee.*

Foolish, when you lose you will not flee. They will take you to confess, and they will sentence you. They will hang you in a square, and they won't take you down until your neck has rotted and your head has fallen off. She turned and sought out the last one. Implacable she shouted at him, *You!* He was the first to enter through the window. The boy looked at her, scared, and Bernadeta said, mercilessly, *They'll shoot you in the head, halfway up the longest and steepest stairs you've ever seen. They will force you to go up and down them, carrying boulders, many men, like ants, bearing rocks up and down, and when you can go no further, you will fall like a sack, a foreign soldier will shoot you in the head, and with a hook they will drag you down the stairs.* She was holding up her belly. Then she added, *You will lose the war! You will lose the war!* And the shortest one, the one who would rot in the square, and the one with the ruddy face and the busted eye, wanted to hurt her. The other two held them back. They called her *whore, witch, madwoman.* And Bernadeta shrieked, but not even she knew whether she was still laughing or whether she was now crying. Inside her eyes, all was black. Black as she had seen that the sky would be when the sun went out with a bang that would kill everything, and it would be night forevermore.

Bernadeta gave birth as she had foreseen she would give birth. Alone. In the kitchen. On the floor. Squatting. With her legs open. Cramped. And her eyes closed. Sweating, grunting, pushing, and lowering hesitant hands that made their way through the dampness and the pitching and the heaving, until they touched the baby's head within. When she touched her she moved. Bernadeta gritted her teeth, and seeing that there was nowhere for her to flee to, she looked the pain in the face. It was a pool of black water. She couldn't see the bottom, and the surface gleamed, oily and freckled with dead insects. She dove in. From within she reached the baby, without screaming, because no one would have heard her. She pulled her out of that sticky gorge, dragging her like a worm, until she was on top of her belly. She was a downy girl, well made, covered in blood and lard. But when Bernadeta looked at her, she shrieked. She placed a hand on her bum, and she bellowed. And that little girl, who didn't yet know that she and her mother were no longer one and the same thing, cried, too, as if the grief were her own. With the same hoarse and terrible cry that ripped through Bernadeta. Because it couldn't be, it couldn't, she told herself, that that warmish infant, whom she would name Dolça, had been born without a tail. There was no possible way it could be, because Bernadeta had seen that she would have a tail. She had seen it. A goat's tail, like her father's, lovely and charming and short and hairy.

Then they bombed Sant Hilari, and Bernadeta was surprised to hear the bombs so close. And when the war ended, the women came. The ones on the losing side. Like vermin. Loaded down with questions. Bernadeta received them in that forsaken kitchen where every tenet of hospitality, order, and cleanliness had been abandoned centuries ago, and she did not offer them anything to drink. She squeezed her eyes like lemons in exchange for a handful of onions, a pillowcase full of vermicelli, a few potatoes, some eggs like a treasure, a ham bone or a piece of bacon. And she told them where their man was. Each of their men. Buried in a hole. What they had done to them, what the winners had done to their sisters and their daughters. Where they had tossed those brothers. Their father. A son. Their cousin, mother of three girls. *They came looking for your sister, but your niece begged them not to take her. And since they were taking her anyway, she went along, because she was just a girl and she didn't think they would kill her too. They executed your son by firing squad and they threw him into a grave with eight other men.* And in the middle of the kitchen in Mas Clavell, the mother cried out, *My son, my son, those who killed you will live to regret it, but you won't. They killed your husband and his brother. They raped them and then they killed them. They piled them up inside a mass grave. First they tortured your son, and when they were finished they shot him.* The women's eyes gushed like terrible springs. *She was shot. They were a group of two women and three men with their hands tied, but they were followed by a young man. The armed men leading them told him to get lost. But when they lined up the detainees, the young man ran and hugged your daughter and wouldn't let go, and since he wouldn't let go, they shot them both in their embrace.*

Upstairs sometimes Dolça screamed like a piglet. She shrieked and yelled, and the women's backs shivered. But her mother wouldn't move. They came to the door forewarned. Bernadeta heard them there, repeating to one another, *Don't let the Lizard touch you. If you let the Lizard touch you, you are done for. And don't look her in the eye. If you look her in the eye, she will see your death.* Because she had been right. She had told those in the revolutionary committee how they would be killed. She had guessed right. And word had gotten around. And she had also told them that they would lose the war, and they had lost. And she had even confessed that before the war broke out, she had been living with the devil! And although none of those four men had believed her at first, now there were those who did. And the women murmured that that girl who shrieked upstairs was deformed, hairy, and ugly, half goat, half girl, because she was the daughter of the He-Goat of Biterna. Others even swore that the revolutionary committee men had found the Evil One hidden inside the house, and that they had taken him to testify in Girona, where he had confessed all the evil things he had done since time immemorial.

And that afterward they'd shot him and cut off his feet, which were rooster feet, and brought them to Barcelona, but that in all the commotion of the war, they'd since been lost. And before they entered the house they would exclaim, *It wasn't Satan! Please, woman. It was a small, minor demon, just following orders. What would Satan possibly be doing in Catalonia?!* And another added that, when they had thrown the footless cadaver into a ditch, her sister-in-law had seen it, and seen that it looked just like a regular man. And they continued, *I don't believe they killed the devil, I don't believe she lived with the devil, Franco is eviler than any devil, Hush, Enriqueta, please.* But they didn't keep quiet. They whispered that the demon's member was as long as an arm. Rough as a grater. Red and purple and with three tips, like three pitchforks, and that was why Bernadeta looked at them with the face of a haughty madwoman who'd just been resuscitated, dying of thirst, and doomed. Because she no longer had any outlet for her basest instincts, the most profound ones, the chasms of pleasure that lodge deep and lead to hell, and that no man can ever fill.

Downstairs, Marta entered the kitchen and went into the pantry. She came out with a sweaty bottle. She opened it and foam poured out. She brought it quickly to her mouth and swallowed a gulp. She squealed with delight. Then she pulled a knife from the drawer, and a board, and she sat down at the end of the table to cut a long, dry sausage into pieces. The women were again at the window. They craned their necks, looked out, got up on tiptoe, and laughed. Marta chopped the sausage, drank, and pulled out her little mirror, and Alexandra's voice, as if it were trapped inside the kitchen, again said, Mama, I can't find my white sneakers, do you know where they are?, Great-Grandma is sleeping and I made sure not to wake her up, we're going to Olot now, mwah. Marta swallowed the sausage she'd been chewing, brought the little mirror up to her mouth, and exclaimed, ay, I don't know where they are, but I'll look, and if I find them I'll let you know. Good night, baby goat, have a good time. Then she put the little mirror on the table, face down, and took another swig. The clatter of the rain was welcoming. Marta looked toward the window, as if she could sense that all the women were bunched up there. Bored of all the waiting. Curious and expectant. Nudging one another with their asses and elbows, smiling and asking: "Do you see him?" But they couldn't see anything, because the night was dark, opaque, quivering, and rainy, made of gray splatters, gloomy patches, and murky shadows. Then Dolça poked her head out from amid the arms and waists of the women. She abandoned the tangle of backs and came running out of the kitchen, crossing the threshold with her mouth agape. First she smelled the goat, then she heard the bleating. The pens were dark. Dolça sensed the gilded coach and, farther back, the bumps that were animals. She felt around and found what she was looking for. She opened up a sack of grain and reached in. She grabbed a handful and trotted back to the kitchen with a full fist. She grabbed a small plate, poured the goat food onto it, and again buried herself in the bustle of hips and necks until she managed to open the window. Then she reached out and placed the plate on the sill, as an offering. She quickly shut the window, and Joana laughed like a mare. The women craned their necks even more and pointed their toes, surveying the darkness between the trees. They were searching for the black stain of an immense bull, the silhouette of a he-goat tempted by the treats, the gleaming eyes of a calico cat, or the curled shape of an ugly man in a storm.

Dolça never did like the weepy women who visited her mother, because they always crossed themselves when they saw her. But she liked their children even less, because they threw rocks at her.

They revealed crooked rows of protruding yellow teeth, and they asked Dolça if her father was a billy goat. They put up fingers behind their heads, like horns. And they told her that her father was the He-Goat of Biterna, and that he'd mounted her witch of a mother, whom they called the Lizard. And they laughed. They added that witches live for a thousand years, and that they were old and ugly, cross-eyed, blemished, and hairy, with missing things or extra things. And they cried out, saying that Dolça had been born with a goat's tail that her mother had cut off with hot pincers. Dolça would say that wasn't true, that she wasn't born with a tail, but they didn't listen. They shouted at her, *I've never seen so many pots for so little fare!* and *When Barcelona was a meadow, Vora-Tosca was a wen!* They chased her, calling, *Goat face, bugaboo, you're uglier than sin! You're uglier than tripping a priest! Hag! Monkey! Mole!* And Dolça ran as fast as her little legs could carry her, because she didn't want them to check to see if she had a tail.

That was why Dolça was so fond of her beloveds. Because they weren't a bunch of kids throwing rocks and shouting invectives, but individual men wooing her with gallantries. Dolça soon understood that when the boys were all together they would say the cruelest things, but taken on their own, they were sweet. And over time they did say many, many sweet things to Dolça. Many more than all the impertinences of all the boys in Sant Hilari. An enormous mountain of flattery, honeyed words, filthy talk, and sweet nothings whispered into her ear. But the fact was that Dolça had had a string of lovers so long you couldn't see the end of it. If she did a roll call, it would never end. Manta and Flabiol, Hurts Here and Baby Jesus, the Bad Hunter, and Little by Little, Filet, Sardina, Sisí, Puça, Mr. Goodafternoon, Regalim, Neula, Lleig, Pantano . . . There were so very many that halfway through the list, Dolça lost her train of thought . . . because she thought that if she had to choose just one out of all her boyfriends, well, there was no way she could ever choose just one. Impossible. Oh no. No way. Forget about it. But if they let her choose two . . . if they let her choose two, then she would choose Lleig and Pantano.

At first, Lleig was just a voice among the trees that said, *Fear me not, miss.* And it was a good idea to warn her, because the man's face was burned and resembled the face of the moon. His more intact cheek was bronzed and leathery and he hadn't shaved in a while. He was strong and corpulent, he wore gray trousers with leather spats and boots, and he asked her in a whisper for a bit of bread and a little salt pork and maybe something for his knee, which had swelled up from all the walking. He also asked, in a feral voice low and hoarse from lack of use, whether she had today's newspaper. She didn't, but she brought him marigold-infused oil and some bread. The man had been hiding in the woods. Dolça watched how he rolled up his trousers and very carefully anointed his muscular calf with its curly hairs, his thick thigh, and his distended knee. His hands were also scorched. Dolça asked him what had happened. It seemed at first that the man was not going to reply. But then Lleig explained that his house had caught fire when he was eight years old and his sister five. His face and hands had been burned and his sister was completely consumed by fire. She'd died. And a few years later, in that selfsame house, which Dolça thought must have been a bad house, a bolt of lightning came through the chimney, trapping his mother and killing her as well. But death hadn't deterred him from fighting, or from having ideas. Not the death of his sister, nor the death of his mother, nor the deaths of all his friends and comrades. *Although the worst of all*, he mused, *isn't dying. Everyone knows death will come for us all one day. The worst of all is the lone-*

liness. Seemed as if it had been years since he'd spoken, but then he got into the swing of it, and Dolça enjoyed his stories of sabotages and holdups, and of timid, wild men hidden in the woods like boars. He told her about the time when death had scared him the most. When some German soldiers killed every single person in that one town. Dolça didn't know where Germany was, and Lleig pointed in its direction: *Thataway.* Lleig and his men had sabotaged a train. Made it derail. Dolça had never seen a train, and he had to describe one for her. She imagined it like a house with small wheels. In retaliation, the Germans had burned down an entire town. And then Lleig, who was the captain, *a captain who peeled potatoes*, and fifty guerrilleros laid seige and annihilated an entire company of German soldiers. But sometimes Lleig still thought about it and he couldn't believe it, two hundred children and two hundred women, burned alive like that. And he told her that he had fought in the war here, and that afterward he'd gone to France, and then he'd fought in the war there. Dolça didn't know where France was either, and the man pointed north: *Thataway.* It was terrible that Dolça knew so little about those wars and the countries that had fought them, the most important wars of the century, he said, because if everybody forgot about the wars, if nobody cared about them and nobody thought about them, then two hundred children and two hundred women could be burned up again, just like that. Dolça looked at his mouth, which was burned only on one side. And the man swore that, foolish as he was, he'd believed, with every drop of optimism he could muster, that when the war was won, that war that wasn't a French war but a world war, the allies would overthrow Franco, too, and fascism would be finished. Dolça stared at his chin now, at the patches that had skin and the patches that didn't. And Lleig warned her that, even though everybody was pretending the war was over, it wasn't. And then Dolça took his burned arms and his hands and placed them around her body, like a coat that smelled of a bonfire. The man with the melted face said to her, *Wait, miss, wait,* but Dolça stroked the patterns like lichen and mosses that came down his neck and chest, and she put his hands back where they had been. When they had finished loving each other, Lleig recited love poems to her in Spanish. They went like this: *I want to have my grave / far from the church grounds / where there are no white blouses / nor gilded pantheons. / I want my grave to be / covered with tall hawthorn, / for all around it to spring up, / grass for the herds, / and for the tired black dog / to rest in my shadow. / I don't want lay clergy or priests / to come to my burial, / and the flowers should be / a bunch of spiky thistles.* Dolça didn't understand such words, but she liked the cadence. Lleig would often sigh and say he was dying for a cigarette. But he'd had to give up smoking, because the lit tip of a cigarette could be seen from a great distance.

Pantano smelled of water tinged with verdigris and Dolça called him Pantano, "Reservoir," because he was helping build a dam between those mountains. He had a thick mustache and was tall and dark, with strong arms and strong thighs from lugging so many rocks and pushing carts endlessly. And he talked and talked, as if his life depended on it. He had a joyful way of speaking, saying things like *My favorite word in your strange language, that's spoken only here in these mountains, because here people live hidden like vermin, is* dolsa. Dolsa, dolsa, dolsa, *so sweet!* He spoke in Spanish, like in Lleig's poems, because he was from a village called Torredonjimeno. Dolça could barely understand him, and he could barely understand her. But Dolça could make out the word *Barcelona* and the word *pantano* and the word *Mateo,* because Pantano had gone to Barcelona to look for work with a friend from his village named Mateo, and someone had asked them, *Do you want to work on a reservoir that they're starting to construct?* But after much time listening to him talk, Dolça began to understand more and more. Pantano explained to her that he and Mateo had taken a train to Vic, and that at the Hotel Colón they'd met up with the man who drove the truck to the dam. They'd had time to spare, and they'd gone to the Plaça dels Màrtirs, and they'd eaten chickpeas. *Garbanzos the way they make 'em here. Cooked with water and strained, and they add a little olive oil and that's it!* And he said that, out on the street, they'd asked a young man what time it was and the boy had said, *Two quarters and a half to two* in Catalan, and Pantano laughed. *I still didn't know what time it was!* But when they got into the truck bed, and they saw the mountains drawing near, so dark and rocky and steep, the two friends thought, *Where are they taking us?* Sometimes Pantano would get mad and exclaim, *The workday at the reservoir is ten and a half pesetas, and overtime is a peseta and a half. A kilo of black bread costs eighteen pesetas, white bread twenty. They give you bread, but they take it out of your weekly wages, and that's how reservoirs are made!* Dolça liked the stories about how they built the reservoir. And about shaking hands: shaking hands meant the workday was over. And about how, when they got back to the barracks, Pantano and Mateo would gather wood, and one would start chopping kindling to build a fire and get started on the meal, while the other would go to the canteen for *rice and potatoes and a salt cod tail.* Pantano's mother was a good cook and she'd taught him to cut the potatoes *like this* if they were for boiling, or *like that* if they were for frying, and it was a good thing he'd learned because now he could put it to use, and Pantano and Mateo ate better than anybody else in those barracks, and the next day there were still plenty of leftovers for lunch on the job. He would kiss her, still talking, not even stopping to catch his breath. *When we got to the reservoir there were barely any tools!*, but luckily it was summer and the weather was nice and they could get by with a blanket, no sheets. *But when autumn came, nobody could get a wink of sleep. I'd never been so cold in my life and I'd never hugged another man before. But I didn't care if they laughed and called me a faggot; I didn't want to freeze to death!* And he said that the first Christmas, his mother had sent him a package with two chorizos, and *that was the happiest moment I'd ever had in these mountains. And we ate them with a liter of wine, and one guy from Córdoba, who we gave some chorizo to, said,* Let's go to midnight Mass, *and so we did. And since in Andalusia people take bottles and wineskins into the church, and drink and sing until Mass starts, we drank and sang until the priest came and told us this isn't a bar for singing and drinking. And we answered that this was how we'd always done it in Andalusia and he replied,* You must have a different God down in Andalusia! *and we were out of there like a shot, and once the dam is finished, that church will be just a home for fish.*

Sometimes he would talk about the dead: *Eleven have died since I got here. And before I arrived, there were at least four more.* He knew one of them very well. Named Hipólito, also from Andalusia. A cart fell on him and crushed him. Pantano, who was in the workshop when he found out that Hipólito had gotten hit by a cart, grabbed a cot and ran out, but when he was almost there they told him, *Don't run, it's too late,* and he turned tail because he didn't want to see Hipólito flattened. Sometimes he would talk about his mother and his sister, who had followed him there. Not up there. No. To Vic. Where his sister worked in a toy factory and his mother was a maid for a man named Siset, who had been the finest matador in Vic. Who would always take off his jacket and say, *This is how I did it with the bulls, like this!* Pantano's little brother was in Figueres, and when he finished his military service he'd go to Vic as well, and that way, said Pantano, when he got them all settled, he'd look for work in the city as a mechanic and never set eyes on these mountains ever again. *I don't know whether people leave here because they're gonna flood it all, or if they're gonna flood it because the people are leaving.*

Looking consummately bored, Marta lifted one butt cheek and farted. Loudly. And the women, who were still pressed up against the window, turned and started shrieking and laughing. To celebrate it. They laughed hoarsely, threw their arms in the air, clapped their hands, their breasts bouncing. They made fart sounds with their mouths and smacked their thighs and the countertop. Marta, unflappable, stood up, abandoned the little empty bottle, and walked out of the kitchen. When the door closed, she turned off the light, and the women were left in the dark by the window, still pissing themselves with laughter.

Beneath Bernadeta's closed eyelids floated a pleasant gray haze, hospitable and consoling. From within that mist, she heard the rain drumming against the roof. The goats bleating. Marta's distant footsteps coming up the stairs, crossing the parlor, growing progressively drawn out and more faint, and then entering the bathroom. Then the sound of hot, vigorous, regulated water inside the house mixing with the clattering of rainwater, rampant, colossal, and cold.

Dolça gave birth in the morning and would die that afternoon. But Bernadeta didn't cry, so as not to scare her. She called her *baby goat* and Dolça got down on her knees. She circled the room on all fours, drenched in sweat, with her hair stuck to her face. Bernadeta pushed Dolça's hair aside, saying, *Sssh, sssh*, and caressing her. Sometimes Dolça wanted to be caressed, other times not. They were squatting and Bernadeta said to her, *Push*, and *You can do it, baby goat*, and *I'm here with you*. And then the little head was out, and Bernadeta exclaimed, *Look at her, look at her.* The baby was round and full, and her eyes were closed and her mouth was open. She looked like a ferret, and they named her Marta. Dolça was a spring that wouldn't stop gushing. A stream of red blood. But Bernadeta didn't look for a midwife, or a doctor of any sort, because she had seen how Dolça would die, and she wanted to be by her side. She bit her lips to keep them from opening and saying that, with all her looking at nasty things for other people, Bernadeta hadn't looked at her girl enough. She was caught by surprise. Dolça had grown up too fast. The way kittens and blackberry bushes do. And she leashed her grief with a very short cord, and she didn't ask Dolça for forgiveness, because Dolça would have forgiven her. She didn't add that there are two miracles in this life—one is being born and the other one is dying—because Dolça was sleepy. Her eyes were closing and her head was falling back. Bernadeta didn't even whisper that she wished they had more time, so she could say again and again how she was the prettiest little baby goat of all, because now Dolça's eyelids were wide open and she was tranquilly looking at the child she'd just given birth to. Dozing. Contented. So Bernadeta kept quiet. Because there are things that can't be said. Because you can talk about misfortune, and you can talk about grief; you can talk about remorse and guilt, and about death, about evil and the things men do. The good things and the bad things. But you can't say how a girl is made. There aren't enough words to explain it, because you made her like dirt makes trees, and trees make branches, and branches make fruit, and fruit makes seeds. In the dark. From a place so deep within that you didn't know you knew how to do it.

A bolt of lightning struck. Bernadeta sensed the blast that glowed red and pink, and she half opened her eyes. But after the flash, all was black. The old woman nodded, patient, like someone greeting an old friend, and the night opened, decipherable and slow. From the darkness emerged the foot of the bed, the walls, the door. The thunder boomed. And the sound of the hot water inside the house stopped. In the bathroom, Marta was making noises; she must've been drying off and getting dressed, because then she came out, and her footsteps crossed the parlor.

Pantano brought a cradle to Mas Clavell and said to Bernadeta, *I'm not the father, ma'am.* Then more men came, like shepherds acting out the nativity scene. Puça brought a doll and said that Marta was pretty. Mr. Goodafternoon brought a rattle and said only *Good afternoon.* Regalim brought some balm but didn't say anything, because he was whimpering. The Bad Hunter brought a rabbit; Filet, a toy car; Sardina, a hat; Baby Jesus, tiny socks; and Lleig didn't come, because the Civil Guard had shot him to death in an ambush. Hurts Here didn't make an appearance either, because he'd fallen ill that winter, and had taken to rest in a house called the Torre de Rupit, but he couldn't cure himself and he had died over Easter week. Manta hadn't shown up either, because his mother had taken him to the spas in Switzerland. And Little by Little was last to arrive, and he brought a goat who had milk because her kid had died of diarrhea. He said, *Goat milk is the closest to woman's milk.* And Bernadeta was pleased when all those men were gone, and that sad animal who was looking for her kid stayed to keep her company. The goat had a long face, clever eyes, a soft, warm snout, thin ears, and horns that grew out of the back of her head. She came and went as she pleased, as if it were her house, and when she chewed indifferently, her mouth opened toward one side and the two tufts on her neck bounced. Bernadeta felt the old clouds of spite gathering within her, how they tried to curl her fingers and gums so the teeth and claws of rage would grow, but she couldn't find the strength to become incensed, and with the little she'd accumulated over years of crawling through the mud of others' misery, she bought more goats. A scrawny herd of healthy animals that got into everything. In every corner of the house, one could be found bleating. And when someone came up to the house with a question, Bernadeta would tell them that she could no longer see the answer, and she would instead sell them a kid or a wedge of cheese. She liked making cheese because it was like making magic. The milk, silently, when you weren't looking, turned into a thick, silky, compact mass that Bernadeta would cut. Then she would stick her arms into that dark bloodlike broth, warm, and white instead of red. A pool of coagulated oblivion, where your hands got lost until you molded it. Then everything dripped. Elbows, sieves, wicker frames, the table. The house reeked of milk, of mold, of dampness. And the cheeses rested. In the dark. Each one like a world that had yet to awaken. Yet to burgeon the fungus that would be its moss, and its underbrush, and the skinny green leaf-sprouts of its trees, and its flowers, and its flying insects, and its creatures, its fish that walked, the ugly frogs, the clumsy toads, the armadillo bugs big as goats, the centipedes like snakes, the lizards like horses, the monstrous hens, the mice, the weasels, the squirrels, dormice, rats, moles, shrews.

The doorframe of Bernadeta's bedroom lit up. And Marta's silhouette crossed through the threshold, enveloped in blue light. The old woman, drifting off, caught a glimpse of her and thought she looked like a fairy who had caught a star in her hand. She called out to her: "Marta."

Marta dazzled Bernadeta and murmured, "The power's out. I'm going to see if it's just us." Her hair was wet and a towel was wrapped around her shoulders.

But Bernadeta reached out toward the gleam and with one

hand beckoned for Marta to enter. To come closer. She wanted to touch her.

Marta would lift the goat kids by the ears. They'd bleat and jump. Headbutt her in the belly. She would reach for their tails, which wagged happily. She would chase them. She would stretch out on the ground and they would climb up on her back. She would drag the adult goats this way and that. She would herd them. She would wrap her arms around them and hang from their necks. She would make them walk on two legs. And she would laugh. With the dark, liquid laugh of a donkey, of a mare, that Bernadeta had heard millions of times, because Marta laughed exactly like Joana did. But Marta didn't know who Joana was. Bernadeta didn't talk about her. Not about Joana, and not about any of the other relatives. Not about what they'd each lacked, nor about the things she could see. Because Marta would've forgotten anyway. That girl had no memory. She had been born without one. She traveled light and carefree. Absentminded. Scatterbrained. And she had been slow to start talking. A fat, sweaty nun from Sant Hilari had walked up to Mas Clavell and said that Marta had to go to school, but the nuns had thought she was dimwitted once she started. Dimwitted because all she did was laugh and say *this* and *that* and *whatchamacallit* when she couldn't remember words, and she expressed herself so imprecisely that it was difficult to understand her. She would say *jar* when she meant *bowl*, she would say *goat* when she meant *dog*, she would say *slice* when she meant *cheese*.

Another flash of lightning. It spread like a spiderweb, lighting up the mountains and the trees. It illuminated the drops of rain, the path, the garden plot, the threshing floor, and the roof. Its light traced the walls inside the house, the furnishings, the bed, the old woman. Marta came into Bernadeta's bedroom and drew close to the window. She looked outside, but the darkness again swallowed everything up. The thunder resounded, muffled, deep, and brutal, and as its bellow made its scattered journey, every other sound was smothered.

Sometimes the goats would escape and the neighbors would bring them back. Bernadeta disliked those farmers and what she saw when she looked at them. The things they had done, and those they hadn't done yet, and how they would die. So she would hide. But Marta found them amusing, those surly men who would say things to her like *Goats are the cows of the poor*. Or *Goats carry the Maltese fever*. Or *When you milk goats, they mutter obscenities*. Or *Goats sin as they please, as evidenced by their bald knees. Their evil thoughts are greatly feared, as evinced by their teeth above their beard. And of their guilt the sign is plain, tails as short as summer rain*. Or *When a goat sneezes, it means the weather will shift*. Sometimes they would let Marta get up onto their tractors and their trailers. And one day she suddenly said, *Everybody has a motorcycle* and *I want one, to race.* If you listened carefully you could hear the buzzing, the grumbling, and the snores, the mountain like an anthill. Marta started working at the intestine processing factory. But then, when she'd saved enough money, she announced, *I'm not going to buy a motorcycle; I'm going to buy myself a car, because now I like rallies better.* She had already met the race car driver. Alexandra's father. Marta had turned up at Mas Clavell with scratches and a black eye, and she'd exclaimed, *They ran me over!* She was laughing. *We were watching the race from a good spot, but there was gravel on the track and one of the cars skidded off and ran into me and a guy from Viladrau. We were thrown into a barrier and had to go to the hospital, so we missed the whole championship. But afterward the driver who hit us gave me his trophy*—she was smiling euphorically—*and invited me to be his copilot tomorrow.* And that love story lasted many years. On again, off again, and on again, again. Bernadeta tried to look only at her goats, but sometimes she caught a glimpse of the driver, how he shook his head, no, I mean it, no. She saw him surrounded by children and another woman. She saw how he left. Marta wasn't crying. She forgot him quickly. But then there would be another race, and she forgot that she'd forgotten him. And they were back together. Again. Even before Marta knew it herself, Bernadeta could see that she was pregnant.

Marta was standing at the window, her eyes wide and gleaming. She stared into the black night. She focused the blue light against the pane, but outside all was dark, and the watery glow couldn't touch anything. She turned toward Bernadeta and said: "I thought I saw a bull on the threshing floor!" And then she laughed. Raucously. And Bernadeta laughed with her.

Marta still worked at the intestine factory, but she no longer raced; now she was part of a local theater group, the same people who, organized the Christmas festivities and who, according to her, put on *the most spectacular Three Kings' parade in the area.* Every year they'd repaint glorious parade floats and distribute them to be stored around town. Marta kept the white king's coach, which was blue and gold, in the goat pen. When they did plays, Marta always asked for small, comic roles; otherwise, she couldn't remember her lines. And Alexandra invariably exclaimed, *No, please, Mama, not again, it's so embarrassing!*, because Alexandra was a serious creature who was nothing like her mother and couldn't stand things that were embarrassing. Even if someone else was doing them. She had been like that, punctilious and severe, since she was a little girl. When Bernadeta got confused and called Alexandra by the wrong name, when she called her *Dolça* or *Marta*, Alexandra would look at her intransigently and rejoin, *My name is Alexandra.* With so much firmness that it seemed impossible for a creature so small to contain it. Then she would ask her, *Great-Grandma, how old are you?* Bernadeta would reply, *Very.* Alexandra sought precision: *But how old, exactly?* Bernadeta would answer, *I don't know*, and the girl would exclaim, *But how can you not know!?* The old woman would mutter, *I lost count*, and Alexandra would shake her head and ask, *Why is everyone in this house so absentminded?!* And she would insist, *But more than a hundred or less? I'd say more.* And the creature couldn't help but say, *You shouldn't have lost count.* But Bernadeta shrugged because, after all, when all was said and done, it was the years who lost count, absentminded, increasingly fleeting, increasingly nimble and unbridled. And in that farmhouse, and on that mountain, and everywhere, if you really thought about it, time had always done whatever it felt like doing. Marta was a woman who already had a daughter, and Alexandra, who'd been a baby in swaddling clothes, was a real girl, with no patience, who found almost everything ridiculous and slapdash. She would say, *What a dumbass!* all the time, in a deep, sharp voice that made you wonder whether being a dumbass was something you wanted to be, or not. She looked like Elisabet, but she didn't know that. She was vain like Dolça. She was constantly taking pictures of herself, pursing her lips and tilting her head. And she was always complaining that Mas Clavell was an old house and that they needed to renovate it, in a tone of voice that would've made Margarida proud. Alexandra was studying something that Bernadeta only half understood, and not only did she not race like her mother, but she didn't even drive, because that strict and impatient little goat invariably got what she wanted, and she always managed to get someone to drive her wherever she needed to go. Now she was dating a guy from Olot, and he would take her around all day long. The two first things that Alexandra had said about that boyfriend was *He has an Audi* and *His house is renovated*. And one day, when Bernadeta was still feeling quite well and the three of them were sitting out on the threshing floor, she'd explained how they'd met when she was working for the town's youth brigade. The work was *super boring* and they made them wear *horrible* orange shirts, but Alexandra had cropped hers so it would be a little less ugly, without asking if she could, because they would've said no, and by the time they told her she couldn't cut it, it would be too late and she would already be showing lots of midriff. And she said, *The first time we spoke, Eloi, who was on vacation with his parents, said he liked my T-shirt. The cropped orange one. And I said,* You're such a dumbass! I look like a butane tank! Marta and Bernadeta laughed, and Marta asked, *You called him a dumbass?* and Alexandra replied, *Of course.*

Marta approached the bed, and Bernadeta took her hand as if she were catching it. She drew her to her chest. And she said, in a hoarse and composed voice that she hadn't used all day, "We've had a good run, Marta, we really did. We've been good company for each other."

And Marta laughed again. More. Her laughter burbled up warm. Vaporous. Enveloping. And it spread to the old woman. Who, with open eyes, scoured the cavernous night. She looked at the heavily laden clouds, the yellow light from the houses, the darkness below the trees. Until she found Alexandra. Hidden in a stretch of forest near Olot, where it wasn't yet raining. When the drops did begin to fall, her friends would open up their mouths and spin around beneath the water. There were half a dozen girls and boys there in the dark. Bernadeta could scarcely make out their faces, all she could glimpse were splotches, bumps, arms, the burning tips of cigarettes, a gleam off a tooth, their breath in the cold air, the clinking of bottles and of earrings. They drank and danced, jumped and shouted, and laughed, and pushed one another, and kissed one another, and got up on one another's shoulders, and fell and got up again. They were a mass of happy bodies, moving together like intoxicated shadows.

Marta, beamish, murmured, "Come on, come on, sleepy time, come on." And the old woman obeyed. She was still smiling. She closed her eyes like a little girl, Marta stroked her, and a thick stupor offered her shelter. The last threads that linked her to consciousness grew wispier and wispier, and severed. And Bernadeta fell asleep.

The entryway and the kitchen were in shadows. The women sat around the table. They lifted their knees and stomped their feet and scratched anything they could get their nails on. Blanca yawned. Elisabet sighed. Àngela snorted. Dolça couldn't hold back anymore and asked, "How much longer now?"

Joana responded, "Not much."

Through the panes on the door they watched the blue light from the little mirror descend the stairs. Marta went to the built-in cabinet in the entryway and illuminated it. She moved switches, and each time she touched them they went cleck, but the darkness won out and the light did not return.

Joana said, "Once upon a time there was a farmer and his wife who lived in a farmhouse surrounded by fields that they themselves had sown. But they had a vast expanse of land, and it was too much for them to handle."

The women shuffled about smugly. Blanca and Àngela leaned back in their chairs. Dolça and Elisabet had their elbows on the table and chins in their hands.

"One morning the farmer went out to survey his fields and he realized that the wheat was already turning golden brown and that soon it would be time for reaping. So he went down to the village to hire some reapers, but when he got there he found that they'd all been hired and he was too late. So the man, downcast and worried, returned home, all the while thinking, Whatever will I do with no reapers?! The wheat is ripe! And my fields so vast! Fie! I've brought this upon myself! He was so agitated that as he walked he muttered aloud, *Where in the blast might I find reapers! I'd offer my very soul to the devil, if he'd reap those fields . . .* Of course, the devil didn't need to be asked twice. He gathered up two more devil pals, and all three appeared before the farmer and said to him, *In need of reapers, sir?* The man could plainly see what they were, their very tails were hanging down!, but since he knew no other way out of his predicament, he thought, Any port in a storm, and he replied, *Indeed I am!* And they made him an offer: in exchange for his soul, they would do all the work he asked of them."

The light on Marta's little mirror made elusive shadows that lengthened in every direction. The cold gleam traveled up and down the entryway, slipped into the kitchen through the panes, and raced over the sink, the window, the table. Joana's deep, scratchy voice continued:

"The next day the three devils said to the farmer, *Off a-reaping we go!* But when they got to the fields, they sat down beneath a fig tree and began to whet their tools. Midmorning, the farmer went to see them and found them still sharpening, and afterward they started lacing up their espadrilles, and the man returned home thinking that the wheat would go to seed. But when he checked in at midday, his eyes wanted to pop out of their sockets, because all the wheat was reaped and stacked. *Look, boss, we've finished!* said the big demon. *Now it's your turn.* The poor man, taken aback, could only think to say, *First let me say farewell to my wife,* and they gave him a day to say his goodbyes."

Marta shrugged and closed the cabinet. She yawned and went upstairs with the contused light of the little mirror, drying her hair with the towel. They heard her enter her room. The rain drummed on the roof. And the women were again left in darkness.

"The farmer, dejected and sorrowful, returned home, and when his wife saw his demeanor, she asked him, *Whatever is the matter with you? I'm in a right fix!* he replied, and he weepily explained the fix he was in, all the while exclaiming, *They tricked me, they tricked me!* But she—whose wits were faster than chain lightning, faster than a greased pig, than a scalded cat, than the devil can fly—responded very calmly, *Come now, don't you fret. When they come looking for you, tell them they haven't finished their work. And then send them to me.*"

The wind wailed. Flurries of water battered the house. The drops came in double time and were more and more impetuous. The lightning tore first the sky, then the trees.

"Early the next day, the three demons showed up at the farmhouse and asked the farmer, *Are you ready?* But the man answered, *Not yet. First my wife wants to see you.* The farmer's wife came out to the threshing floor and asked, *Are these the hired hands? Let's just see if they work as well as you said they do.* And she took each of them aside in turn. She sent the first to the well to carry up all the water. And she lent him a basket to bring it to the house. She gave the second one a kidskin, and told him to go to the river and wash it until it was good and white. And she put her baby son in the arms of the third, and ordered the demon to teach him church doctrine. When dusk fell, she went to see them. She reached the well and asked the first demon, *So? How's the work going?* But the devil replied angrily, *I don't know how to do it! As soon as I get the water out of the well, it falls back inside! I quit!*, and he ran furiously toward hell."

The circle around the table added to the uproar of the storm.

The women shrieked and laughed, banged their hands and stomped their feet.

"The farmwife went to the river to see the second demon. *So? How's the work going?* she asked, but the demon replied, *Awful! The more I scrub, the blacker the hide turns!* And he fled in a fit of rage."

Dolça, Blanca, Elisabet, and even Àngela roared. They barked and mewled, they bleated, they clucked, clacked, champed, peeped, grunted, mooed, croaked, neighed, howled.

"The woman searched for the third demon, and found him cursing through his teeth. When she asked him, *So? How's the work going?*, he responded, with smoke coming out of his ears, *You'll have to find another laborer for this job, lady. Hard as I try, this child won't speak! And to top it all off, the church words make my tongue curl!* And he, too, went back to hell, seething with fury."

In the kitchen the women's clamor continued. "Woof-woof, mew, meow, baaah, cluck-cluck, chirp-chirp, oink-oink, cock-a-doodle-do, hee-haw, hee-haw, whoo-whoooo, moooo, aaah-woooooo."

Joana continued, "The farmwife went to find her husband, who was anxiously waiting, and when he realized what she'd done, he was so happy he was bursting out of his skin, and they danced and leapt and laughed."

And the women also danced and leapt and laughed. Until, in the midst of the blackest darkness and the happiest shrieks, Joana's deep, scratchy voice said, "Let us set the table, for we are on the cusp."

The women suddenly stood up and were silent. Joana added, "Let us light the candles." And they lit the candles. "Let us spread a clean tablecloth." And they spread a clean tablecloth. "Let us set the plates and silverware." And they set the plates and silverware. And the napkins. And the cups with blue stems. And they took the lids off the gravy stew, and the fritters, and the forcemeat, and the offal. They took a step back and proudly admired the set table. And Joana, with a toothless, cavernous smile, murmured, "It is time."

The women whistled softly and clapped their hands soundlessly. They lined up and went out. They traversed the entryway like caterpillars. One behind the other. They were an eager procession, looking upward as they climbed the stairs. Joana leading, then Dolça, Elisabet, Blanca, and Àngela. They reached the parlor. They went into the bedroom, where Margarida was expecting them. They encircled the bed in the dark, creating a ring. The rain pounded deafeningly, like drums on the roof. The women whispered impatiently. Margarida went, *Sssh!*, resigned. Bernadeta was a black stain that snored. The snore was nasal, muffled, and serrated. Some of the women giggled, for snoring can be funny. Another bolt of lightning flashed. The white light illuminated the bed and the old woman sleeping in it, with her eyelids closed and her face tranquil, as if she knew where she was going. And the thunder soon echoed, guttural and immense, as if it were inside the very house. Then the darkness returned, and only the sound of water was heard. Bernadeta was no longer snoring. She stuck out her chin. She lifted her eyebrows. She parted her lips. And the women encircling the bed joined hands.

AUTHOR'S NOTE

Many of the stories and legends that appear in this novel, including "The Fart Herb," "The Three Lazy Brothers," and "The Man Who Gave Himself to the Devil," also known as "The Three Devils," are taken from the books *Folklore del Lluçanès* by Josep M. Vilarmau i Cabanes, and *El folklore de Rupit i Pruit*, both published by the Grup de Recerca Folklòrica d'Osona (a research group comprised of Jaume Aiats i Abeyà, Ignasi Roviró i Alemany, and Xavier Roviró i Alemany). I first read the story "L'hostal de la Lletja" (in which a woman manages to break a pact with the devil, thanks to the fact that her husband is missing a pinkie toe) in *Montseny: Històries i llegendes* by Xavier Roviró i Alemany. To learn more about the legends of the Guilleries region, I found the book *Històries de les Guilleries*, also by Xavier Roviró, and the article "Les Guilleries: Terra de refugi" by Josep Tarrés i Turon, very useful, among other sources. To construct the character of Clavell and his band, I consulted sources that included *Serrallonga: El bandoler llegendari català* by Xavier Roviró i Alemany; *Proceso instruido contra Juan Sala y Serrallonga, lladre de pas (salteador de caminos), estractado en su parte más interesante por Juan Cortada, Joan Serrallonga: Vida i mite del famós bandoler* by Joan Reglà and Joan Fuster; *Serrallonga: El bandoler, les seves dones i la justícia* by

Isabel Graupera and Lluís Burillo; and the blog *Serrallonga 1640*. Essential to my work on the character of Miquel Paracolls from Malla was the research undertaken with the assistance of the Episcopal Archive and Library in Vic.

My investigation into the figure of the devil, the pact, and Margarida's descent into hell was greatly helped by the following: *El diable és català* by Sylvia Lagarda-Mata; the project *El simbolisme del pacte amb el dimoni en les llegendes catalanes: Una mostra de transmissió ideològica en l'imaginari català* by Pilar Juanhuix Tarrés; *Dimonis: Apunts de Jacint Verdaguer a la Casa d'Oració*, edited by Enric Casasses; as well as *Visio Tnugdali*, attributed to Brother Marcus, and the descriptions of hell by Josefa Menéndez in *Un appel à l'Amour*.

The character of Pantano is inspired by Félix Jurado's *Memorias de un niño de la guerra (1936–1939) escritas cuando me jubilé, dedicadas a la madre de mis hijos, Lucía Escobar Fernández*, which I discovered thanks to the book *Història de la construcció del Pantà de Sau* by Joan Lagunas. The verses that Lleig recites to Dolça are from a poem attributed to Ramon "Caracremada" Vila Capdevila.

Most of the recipes are drawn from the cookbooks *Llibre de Sent Soví (o Llibre de totes maneres de potatges de menjar)* and *Llibre del Coch (o Llibre de doctrina per a ben servir, de tallar y del art de coch ço es de qualsevol manera, potatges y salses compost per lo diligent mestre Robert coch del Serenissimo senyor Don Ferrando Rey de Napols)*.

And, finally, I must mention, among other sources, the article "Llevadores, guaridores i fetilleres: Exemples de sabers i pràctiques femenines a la Catalunya medieval" by Teresa Vinyoles i Vidal and Pau Castell Granados; the article "Festes i 'alegries' baixmedievals" by Teresa Vinyoles i Vidal; as well as the doctoral thesis "Orígens i evolució de la cacera de bruixes a Catalunya (segles XV–XVI)" by Pau Castell Granados; the books *El llop i els humans: Passat i present a Catalunya* by Josep Maria Massip i Gibert; *The Magical Universe: Everyday Ritual and Magic in Pre-Modern Europe* by Stephen Wilson; *Les arrels llegendàries de Catalunya* by Xavier Fàbregas; the article "Collformich: Relació històrica dels successos ocorreguts des del dia 8 al 11 de gener de 1874, amb motiu de l'entrada dels carlins a Vic," which was published anonymously but is believed to have been written by Josep Gudiol i Cunill; and *Emboscats: La guerra dels que no hi van anar* by Esther Miralles.

ACKNOWLEDGMENTS

Boundless gratitude to Oscar Holloway, Mikel Aboitiz, Marta Garolera, Jan Ferrarons i Llagostera, Nil Prats, Xavier Roviró i Alemany, Mercè Sáez, Francesc Solà, Joan Sáez, Isabel Obiols, Silvia Sesé, Marina Penalva, María Lynch, Mara Faye Lethem, Alexandra Laudo, Lluís Bassaganya, Isa Basset, Jordi Coma, Nadina Latorre, Cristina Oliver, Ignasi Roviró, Jaume Coll, Jaume Coll pare, Maria Màriné, Sebastien Roueche, Albert Grabulosa, Paula Fonollà, Cristina Grau, Gerard Canals Puigvendrelló, Aina Orriols, Àngels Rovira, Francesca Rizzi, Concepció Garcia, Ricard Dilmé i Burjats, Krisztina Nemes, Clara Cortadelles, Martí Sancliment, Mercè Paracolls, Rosa Maria Paracolls, Rafel Ginebra i Molins, Pol Serrahima, Joan Pastoret, Josep Serra, Pau Cardellach, Pius Pujades, Montse Cordero, Nicolás Gaviria, and the Pérez-Izquierdo family.

This novel received a 2020 Literary Creation Grant from the Catalan government and was supported by a 2020 Barcelona Prize grant from the municipal government.

While writing this book, I was a writer-in-residence at the Alan Cheuse International Writers Center at George Mason University (Virginia), the Writers Art Omi–Ledig House program (New York), Faberllull (Olot), the Santa Maddalena Foundation (Tuscany), and the Finestres Literary Residence (Palamós). To all these initiatives, and to all those who are part of them and make them possible, thank you.

PERMISSION ACKNOWLEDGMENTS

Keep in touch with
Granta Books:

Visit granta.com to discover more.

GRANTA

WHEN I SING, MOUNTAINS DANCE

Irene Solá

Translated by Mara Faye Lethem

'Utterly universal . . . and profoundly moving' Max Porter

'Wonderful . . . Timeless and unique' Mariana Enríquez

High in the mountains, Domènec is struck by lightning while out foraging. He and his family – his wife, Sío, and their children, Mia and Hilari – grow up wild on the hulking summits of the Pyrenees, but the land is not theirs. It belongs to those who have long called the mountain their home: chanterelle mushrooms and roe deer, the ghosts of Spain's civil war and the clouds that top these perilous climbs. As the years tumble by after Domènec's death, these inhabitants come together to bear witness to the tragedies that befall the family he leaves behind.

A fiercely imaginative, elemental story of love and loss –
in this time, and in all of time – *When I Sing, Mountains Dance*
is a giddy paean to the land in all its interconnectedness.

'An act of revolutionary revitalisation' Ali Smith

'Magnificent . . . a creepy, earthy masterpiece' Camilla Grudova

'Funny, intimate and sad . . . This attentive, playful, responsive
novel makes an excellent case for stopping and listening' *Guardian*